A TRUNK OF MURDER

TRASH TO TREASURE COZY MYSTERIES, BOOK 5

DONNA CLANCY

SUMMER PRESCOTT BOOKS PUBLISHING

Cool, crisp air, colorful landscapes, and full apple trees are a few of the things that make Autumn my favorite time of year.
Scary Halloween decorations, dark graveyards and ghost hunting add to the festivities of the season.
To all those who enjoy this time of year and all that it brings.

CHAPTER ONE

"I love autumn," Sage said, slipping a sweater over her head. "Cool, but not cold and I get to wear all my big, comfy sweaters."

"I don't know. I'm kind of partial to Christmas and the white landscape glistening in the sun," Gabby replied. "And the colorful festive lights"

"I like Christmas, but I love Halloween even more. There's just something about skeletons, black cats, and spider webs hanging around the house that makes me happy."

"You have two cats now who might like your decorations even more than you do," Gabby said, laughing.

"You're right. I may have to hang all my scary

things a little higher this year to keep them out of their reach," Sage commented.

"I made a thermos of hot apple cider to take with us," Gabby said, setting it in the front console of Sage's van. "I bought it fresh at Cliff's family farm yesterday."

"Speaking of, are you going there this weekend and help set up the haunted hayride?"

"I'm working at the salon all weekend, but I told Cliff I would pop on over on Monday to help with anything left over that has to be done," Gabby said. "The weekends are my busiest time even with the two additional hairdressers I hired."

"It seems to have paid off hiring the manicurist and pedicurist from Madame's shop for your own shop. Now that you are full serve it seems your business has tripled," Sage commented.

"It has. Brenda and Stephanie are so nice. They are great with the customers, too. People are coming all the way from Moosehead to use the salon. I'm so glad I built the addition when I did."

"If things keep up the way they are, you may have to build another addition on the building," Sage said smiling. "Are you ready to get dirty?"

"I am. Is it true Mrs. Perkins said no one has been in the old barn for over forty years?"

"When she called, she told me the last one in the barn was her husband. And he ran off with his young girlfriend a little over forty years ago," Sage answered.

"I can't believe she stayed and worked the farm by herself," Gabby said, climbing up into the van. "If my husband embarrassed me the way he did her, I would have moved far away where no one knew me."

"Marie Perkins is a strong, independent woman. She knew he was having an affair as did everyone in town. I think she was probably relieved when the two lovers left. She stayed put and ran a successful farm until she retired ten years ago."

"I've missed her pumpkin fields. My family always went there to walk the fields and find the biggest pumpkins we could to carve our jack-o-lanterns for the front porch."

"At least we still had Fulton Farms to get pumpkins and apples from once Perkins Farm closed down," Sage said, putting the van in gear.

"True, and all the other goodies they sell there," Gabby replied.

"Mrs. Perkins said there are a bunch of apple crates in the barn among the other furniture and odds and ends we can help ourselves to," Sage said. "I can make some great coffee tables and end tables from apple crates. And if there is a large amount of them, I'm sure Cliff could always use them at Fulton's farm."

"You did bring some work gloves for us to wear?" Gabby asked. "I don't need to get bitten by spiders or any other critters who might be hiding in forty years' worth of dust and clutter."

"I brought nice thick gloves and duct tape to put around the bottom of our pant legs and at the end of our sleeves. You should be well protected," Sage said. "Here's the road."

Apple Tree Lane which led to the farm was long and winding. Apple trees lined one side of the road and gone-by blueberry bushes were on the other side. A little further up, just past the blueberry bushes were empty fields where the pumpkins used to be grown. Now, after ten years of not being worked, the fields were just flat acres of dirt as far as the eye could see.

"I wonder what will happen to the farm if something happens to Mrs. Perkins," Gabby said, sighing. "She has no family to pass it to. I'd hate to see this beautiful land fall into the hands of some developer."

"I heard some developer from Moosehead had already tried to buy the land from her and she refused to sell it to him," Sage said. "She's smart and feisty and I'm sure she has already made some kind of arrangements to protect the land."

"Wouldn't it be awesome if someone bought the land and opened a Christmas tree farm?" Gabby asked.

"Have you been talking to Cliff?"

"No, why?' Gabby asked.

"Because he and I were talking about that very subject the other night over supper. He wants to take part of the Fulton Farm acreage and grow Christmas trees," Sage replied.

"Smart man. Everyone can use a Christmas tree and the only ones that sell them in Cupston are the scouts and the local church. There isn't much left to pick from if you don't get there on opening day," Gabby stated.

"Even if he does put the plan into action, it will be years before the trees are ready to sell."

"It's still a great idea as far as I'm concerned."

"Here we are," Sage said, pulling up in front of the small farmhouse. "Check out the size of the barn behind the house."

"I think it's going to take us a lot longer than one day to go through the place. It's huge," Gabby replied.

"Good thing we came early in the morning to

start," Sage said, hopping down out of the van. "That's odd."

"What?"

"The front door is wide open to Mrs. Perkins' house."

"I hope she's okay," Gabby said.

"Mrs. Perkins! It's Sage and Gabby. Are you okay?" Sage yelled into the house.

No answer.

"Mrs. Perkins! Where are you?" Gabby yelled.

"What's all the fussing about?" Mrs. Perkins asked, coming from behind the house.

"We were afraid something happened to you. Your door was wide open and…"

"I always leave my front door open when it's nice out. Changing the air inside is a good thing to do. It keeps you healthy."

"Aren't you afraid of bugs getting into the house?" Gabby asked.

"Nah, they'll find their way out again if they do," the older woman replied.

"I guess," Gabby mumbled.

"Are you ready to dig through the barn? My husband, the cheating oaf, was the last one to use the place. I never went in there again after he ran off with his young missy," Mrs. Perkins stated. "It was all his stuff, and I had no use for it. I had my own barn built for my farm equipment. That's it over yonder."

"So it's true. We are the first ones to go in there in over forty years?" Gabby asked.

"That's right. The day after Roger left I put a lock on the barn door, and it hasn't been opened since. Here's the key. It's been hanging on a hook at the back door. And Sage, if you see anything you think that handsome boyfriend of yours can use on the Fulton Farm you take it for him and his family."

"If there is that much stuff in there we might have to make more than one trip. My van can only hold so much," Sage said, laughing.

"You make as many trips as you need to. The contents aren't going anywhere, and you can keep the key with you to come and go as you please. Everything has to go one way or another. I don't want the person who takes over the property to have to deal with all this stuff."

"Are you thinking of selling your farm?" Sage asked.

"Oh, no, my dear, but we all have to die someday. This is my home, and I will stay here until the very end. Have fun digging around. I'm going to run into town and will be gone for a few hours. I have errands to do and a meeting at the church," she said, heading for her old truck.

"Aren't you going to close your door?' Gabby asked.

"I haven't locked the place since I lived here, so why start now? Tootles!"

The two friends watched the elderly woman swing her truck around and head off down the long driveway leaving a trail of dust as she went.

"I hope I'm as chipper as her when I reach her age," Sage said. "Shall we go see what's hidden in the time capsule?"

"I think this could prove interesting. I may even find an antique or two for my house," Gabby replied. "Lead the way!"

Surprised the lock opened so easily after all the years of being out in the elements, they stepped into the barn and looked around. The roof was still intact, as were the walls. When the light from the door flooded the interior, a rat shot by Gabby's feet, and she let out a shriek.

"I hate those things," she said, grabbing a rake handle that stood against the wall next to her.

"We are intruding in their space," Sage replied. "Put your gloves on and I'll seal your sleeves closed. Just be careful when you move things around."

"Did you bring any flashlights?"

"I did, but I left them in the van," Sage replied. "Be right back."

"You're not leaving me alone in here with those rats," Gabby said, following her friend outside. "I'll wait right here util you get back."

"Chicken," Sage said, teasing her friend.

"Call me what you want but I'm not going back in there without a strong light beam to guide the way."

Sage returned and the two friends ventured back in now that they could see a good portion of the area around them. Just inside the door they duct taped the bottom of their pant legs closed so now unwanted spiders or bugs could crawl up them. They repeated the same process with their sleeves and then put on heavy-duty work gloves to protect their hands.

"Where do we start?" Gabby asked.

"You start on that side, and I'll start over here. Holler if you find the apple crates," Sage replied.

The two separated. Within minutes, Gabby let out a squeal.

"Are you okay?" Sage asked, thinking her friend stumbled upon more rats.

"Oh, I'm fine. As a matter of fact I'm more than fine. Guess what I found and am claiming?" Gabby answered.

"Must be an antique for your house."

"Remember when you converted those carriage lanterns, and I wanted them for either side of my fireplace, but you sold them to another client? I found two lanterns just like those that you can convert for my house," Gabby said, happily, holding up the pair.

"Set them outside the door and keep digging. We have a whole barn to go through," Sage said. "I found a few apple crates over here, but the way Mrs. Perkins was talking I don't think it's all of them."

"I found a couple, too. I think they are spread all over the barn and not just in one particular place. I'm going to move these outside," Gabby replied.

Within an hour, twenty or so apple crates had been placed in a pile outside the door. Gabby had already placed the lanterns on the front seat floor of the van to make sure they weren't lost in the shuffle. One of the crates had been set aside for holding wiring and smaller parts that Sage had cannibalized for her flipping projects.

"This place is amazing," Sage said. "I found a whole dining set and six end tables I can redo and flip. And I just started digging through this pile."

"I just found another pile of apple crates. Maybe we should load the crates and make the first trip with just those. We can empty them in your storage trailer and come back for some of the furniture," Gabby suggested.

"Good idea. It's still early enough that we can get at least two or three more trips in before it gets dark."

They loaded the van and even had room for some of the smaller pieces of furniture Sage had already found. Sage locked the barn and they left for her shop. They emptied the van setting all the apple crates at the very back of the storage trailer making sure they were organized so as to leave plenty of room for the rest of the items that would be arriving with each trip from the farm.

Returning to the barn, they found another pile of apple crates. Sage called Cliff to see if he wanted to come out with his truck and claim the pile of crates for his family farm. That way, she could fill her van with furniture instead of crates, He said he would be there within the hour.

"Look at this bedroom suite. Why would the Perkins put all this furniture out here?" Sage asked.

"Because when we bought the farmhouse, it was fully furnished," Mrs. Perkins answered from the door. "We had all our own things so everything from the previous owners ended up out here in the barn. Over the years things got piled in front of the stuff and it was forgotten."

"Do you want to look through what we are taking before we take it? Just in case some of your personal belongings got mixed in with the previous owner's things?" Sage asked.

"Sweetie, if it's been out here for all these years and I didn't need it then, I sure don't need it now. You take everything and anything you want," she replied.

"Cliff is coming over with his truck to take some of the apple crates for his farm," Sage said. "I hope you don't mind I asked him to come over and help himself."

"I'm glad you did. I need to talk to your young man about something and I don't want to put it off any longer," Mrs. Perkins said. "Would you have him come to the house to see me when he gets here, please?"

"I sure will."

"Get back to work. You still have a whole barn to go through," the elderly woman said, turning and walking away.

"She wouldn't even come into the barn," Gabby stated. "It must hold only bad memories for her."

"Maybe with us taking away the material items in here she can deal with the building itself and not all their memories."

"There is no way we can take away everything in this barn," Gabby said.

"You're right. But I'm sure Mrs. Perkins has something in mind for what we don't take. She said she wouldn't leave stuff around for the next owner to have to deal with."

"I wonder who the next owner will be. I hope it's someone local and not an out of state developer," Gabby said, sighing. "They've already built up the northern side of Cupston with their condos and housing. I hope the new owner keeps this farmland like it is now."

"Unfortunately, we have no control over what happens with the farm," Sage said, frowning. "Oh well, back to work now that we have an empty van to fill up again."

"Are you going to take the bedroom suite?" Gabby asked, shoveling lamp parts into a box.

"I think I will. I can always flip bedroom furniture and make it more modern for present day décor."

"It looks like there is a lot more of their furniture back here in this corner," Gabby said, climbing over a pile of apple crates. "And a ton more apple crates."

"When Cliff gets here and empties some of the crates out of the barn it might make things a little easier to move around," Sage replied, walking past

Gabby holding an old sewing machine table. "This place has so many old treasures."

A horn sounded outside.

"I think Cliff is here," Gabby said.

"Hello! Where is everyone?" Cliff said from the door of the barn.

"We're in here. Come on in," Sage answered.

"Wow! Look at all the apple crates. My dad will go nuts when he sees them," Cliff said, looking around.

"And we already took a load of them to my storage trailer, so all that you see you can claim for your farm," Sage replied. "But before you start loading them, Mrs. Perkins wants you to go up to her house. She needs to talk to you about something."

"Any idea what?" he asked.

"She didn't say. Just that she needed to talk to you," Sage said, heading for the door with an armload of old barrel rings. "When you get back, we'll help you load the crates."

"Do you want these old plant stands?" Gabby asked.

"Yes, ma'am. They make awesome end tables," Sage replied.

"There're some old sea trunks over in the back corner. You might want Cliff to help load them into the van before he leaves,' Gabby suggested to her friend. "They're kind of bulky."

"Are they empty?"

"I'll check," she answered, climbing over a pile of old tractor tires.

Making neat piles of old barrel staves which must have at one time been complete barrels with the rings she had already loaded into the van, she picked up the first pile and headed for the door.

I can make some awesome wall hangings with these.

As she reached the door, Gabby let out a blood curling shriek behind her.

"Sage, help me! Dead person! Get me out of here!"

CHAPTER TWO

"Hold on, I'm coming," Sage replied, dropping the staves when she heard the fear in her friend's voice.

Gabby continued to scream incoherently.

Cliff and Mrs. Perkins heard Gabby yelling all the way up at the house and had come running to see what was going on in the barn. Cliff ran inside while Mrs. Perkins stopped at the door. Sage was in the process of climbing over the piles of stuff to get to her friend. Cliff followed close behind. Gabby had plastered herself against the wall in the far corner, all the color drained from her face. She was pointing at one of the sea chests.

"In there…in there," she said, repeating herself.

"This one?" Sage asked.

"Yes, there's a body in there. Or what's left of one anyway."

"Are you sure it's not Halloween decorations? They could have stored them in the trunk," Sage asked as she reached to open the one in question.

"What's going on?" Cliff asked.

Sage opened the lid and they both peered in. Sure enough, there was a skeleton of what looked to be a man judging by the clothes which were wrapped around the bones.

"What did you find?" Mrs. Perkins asked from the doorway.

"You better go call the sheriff," Cliff advised her. "There's a body in an old sea chest back here and by the looks of the crack on the skull it looks like the person was murdered and stuffed in there."

"A body? I'll call the sheriff right away," the elderly woman said, running for the house.

"It would have been quicker if we used our cell phone," Sage said.

"It's her farm and she should be the one to make the call," Cliff replied. "I wonder if it's Roger Perkins."

"Are you saying the whole story about him skip-ping town with his young girlfriend was made up and he's been sitting in that trunk since the day he supposedly disappeared?" Gabby asked. "Do you think Mrs. Perkins killed her own husband?"

"This stuff at the back of the barn belonged to the previous owners before the Perkins bought the property. Besides, if Mrs. Perkins killed her husband and hid him in here, why would she give us free rein of the barn now to take what we wanted?"

"Sage is right. If she did kill him and closed the barn all these years it would have made more sense to keep it locked up until she passed, and nothing could have been done about the murder," Cliff said. "Maybe this body is tied to the previous owners and Mrs. Perkins didn't even know it was in here."

Police sirens sounded in the distance. Mrs. Perkins had returned to the door of the barn and this time she stepped inside. She was wringing her hands and sighing deeply.

"Mrs. Perkins, are you okay?" Cliff asked.

"I'm fine. This is so disturbing knowing there was a person in my barn all this time and I didn't know it. This was Roger's barn. How do I know he didn't do this before he left me?"

A cruiser rolled up and shut off its siren. Sheriff White and Deputy Andy Bell exited the vehicle. Cliff walked out to meet them and explain what was found in the barn.

"Mrs. Perkins," the sheriff said, tipping his hat as he passed her following Cliff.

Sage had moved some of the tires and cleared a path to the chest. The sheriff opened the lid and peered in. The bones were enclosed in what was left of a red flannel shirt and a pair of jean overalls. The skull had sagged to the side, up against the side of the trunk and a definite crack could be made out on the back of the bone. A glimmer of gold lit up as the sheriff played his flashlight beam over the inside of the trunk.

"What do we have here?" the sheriff said, taking out a pen and using it to lift a gold chain out of the front pocket of the overalls. "Bell, grab me some gloves out of the car!"

Sheriff White pulled on the gloves and pulled on the chain. Whatever had been attached to the end in the pocket was gone.

"Do you think this is Roger Perkins?" Sage asked. "He supposedly left town with his mistress. How could he end up here in the barn?"

"I recognize that chain. It held a pocket watch I gave to Roger over fifty years ago. It was a beautiful gold watch with a raised relief of a tractor on the front. He always carried it with him no matter where he went. Dressed up or out in the fields plowing, he always had it in his pocket. Is that Roger in the box?" Mrs. Perkins asked, coming up behind the group.

"How long has it been since you've been in here, Marie?"

"I locked the door the day after Roger left me and haven't been in here since. I built my own barn because this one held such bad memories for me. You don't think I killed my husband and stuck him in here, do you? Seriously?"

"First off, we aren't even sure this is Roger Perkins. Secondly, I'm not accusing you of anything. I'm just asking the questions I need to ask," Sheriff White explained.

"I think I need to sit down. I'm going outside and get some fresh air," Marie Perkins stated. "I'll be sitting on the porch swing when you need me."

"Do you really think Marie killed her husband?" Cliff asked the sheriff when Marie was out of earshot.

"I was saying earlier I didn't think she would have opened up the barn to us to search through and take what we wanted if she knew there was a body hidden out here, much less her husband's body, do you?" Sage asked.

"Maybe she forgot it was here. She is getting older. Maybe she started the story way back when that he left and let everyone think that way all these years," Gabby stated.

"My dad was the sheriff back then. I was a young boy, but I remember him talking about the case. I always thought it was funny that Roger disappeared, but his mistress only left town for a few days."

"Who was his mistress?" Sage asked.

"Lucy Winters."

"The Miss Winters who owns the Purple Petunia Florist Shop in town?" Cliff asked. "I never would have seen that coming."

"My dad questioned her. She stated Roger left town without her and she didn't know where he had gone. Lucy was heartbroken to be left behind. She really loved him," the sheriff replied.

"Why did she leave town?" Sage asked.

"She had gone to the motel up in Bridgeton where they used to secretly meet and where they were going to meet to leave together. Lucy stayed there for three days hoping Roger would show up, but he never did so she returned home. My dad said she never married because she never got over Roger."

"That puts us right back to Marie killing her husband. Maybe she snuck up behind him and smacked him in the head the night he was getting ready to leave," Cliff said. "Maybe it was an accident, and she lost her temper."

"It still doesn't make any sense. I can't see her opening the barn to us," Sage replied.

"I'm going to put a call into the M.E. to come pick up the body. We are still not sure if this is even Roger Perkins. The watch chain makes it kind of hard to come to any other conclusion, but we will see," the sheriff said. "Don't touch anything in the area. As a matter of fact, I think your day of digging around in here is over. This is now a crime scene. Everyone needs to vacate the building."

"You'll let me know when I can come back in and resume my treasure hunting, won't you?" Sage asked.

"I will. Now, everyone, outside as I need to go up to the house and talk to Marie while I wait for them to come get the body," the sheriff replied.

"I'm not coming back here. One skeleton is enough for me, thank you," Gabby stated.

The group of friends stood near their vehicles while they watched the sheriff and deputy head up to the house to talk to Marie. The van was only half full and Cliff hadn't loaded any of the apple crates he had come to get.

"I'd say let's load the apple crates piled up outside, but they probably will be gone over by the crime team before they can be removed," Sage said. "I'll be right back. I have to ask the sheriff if I can take the things already loaded into my van."

Several minutes later Sage returned with the okay to take what she had already packed but to keep them in a separate area in her storage unit in case they had to be searched.

"Who's hungry?" Cliff asked. "Pointers is just up the road, and their fried clams are calling my name. My treat."

"I guess we all have a little time to kill now that we have been kicked out of the barn," Sage said. "I could go for one of their fifties burgers."

"Good choice of words," Cliff said, laughing. "Gabby, are you hungry?"

"When aren't I hungry?" she replied, smiling.

"I wasn't sure. You did find the skeleton and all."

"Skeleton or not, I am always up for food especially if someone else is footing the bill," Gabby answered. "What are we waiting for?"

They passed the M.E.'s wagon on the way out. Pointers was busy, so the trio sat at a table on the outdoor patio and waited for their waitress to take their order.

"I can't believe all these years everyone thought

Roger Perkins ran off with his mistress," Gabby said, perusing the menu.

"We still don't know the skeleton is him," Sage replied. "The big question is if Marie didn't kill him and put him in there, who did?"

"If I didn't know Marie as well as I do, I would have to say all the evidence points to her committing the murder," Cliff said. "What I don't understand is why you would stick him in the barn in a box when you have acres of land where you could bury him."

"That would make more sense if you didn't want the body found," Gabby agreed, closing the menu and setting it down.

"Everyone know what they want?" the waitress asked, walking up to their table.

Cliff ordered a fried clam platter, fries, and a side of coleslaw. Sage ordered the fifties burger, medium, with the secret sauce, lettuce, pickles and tomatoes. She also ordered a side of onion rings. Gabby went with scallop roll off the special board. They all agreed to split a pitcher of sun tea which Pointers was well-known for.

"Not to change the subject," Sage said after the waitress left to place their order. "Did you get to talk to Mrs. Perkins before the skeleton was found?"

"I did. She's worried about some developer

getting their hands on her land should something happen to her. She wanted me to recommend an attorney that I trusted to help her with her final wishes. I told her to call Bill Zarian. My dad uses him for all our farm issues and is well versed in wills and business law."

"We were talking about that on the way to the farm this morning," Gabby said. "I think you should purchase some of the land and open a Christmas tree farm."

"Did you tell her we were talking about me starting a tree farm?" Cliff asked Sage.

"I never said a word. She came up with the idea all by herself," Sage replied, pouring a glass of tea for everyone from the pitcher the waitress had just dropped off to them.

"I can't afford to buy Marie's land, but I was seriously thinking of using some of the back acres on the family farm and planting some trees, Cliff said.

"I think it's an awesome idea. Christmas trees never go out of style and almost everyone in Cupston needs one during the holidays," Gabby replied.

"My dad and I are looking into it. There are ten acres which can be used, and we sent out the soil to be tested to see if the area is a fit for planting the trees," Cliff stated. "They said it would be a few weeks before we got the results back."

"I think the new venture is exciting," Sage said. "You could have Halloween Hayrides and the maze and then at Christmas you could have the same hayride decorated for Christmas. The lights would be fantastic."

"The Halloween Hayride is a lot of work. A Christmas one would be well in the future."

"It is a lot of work, I agree. You know me, always looking at the future and voicing my ideas. It would be cool though," Sage replied. "Has your family finally settled on which charity will receive the fifty percent of the proceeds from the hayride this year?"

"You know my mom, she's all about animals, so we decided this year the money would be donated to the local 4H to help kids learn about and take care of farm animals. My mom was ecstatic with the decision."

"Nice," Gabby said, watching the waitress set her scallop roll down in front of her. "These scallops smell heavenly."

"Do you need another pitcher of tea?" the waitress asked.

"That would be great," Sage replied. "And some ketchup, please."

"Are you seriously going to eat all those clams?" Gabby asked Cliff, staring at the mound of bellied clams in front of him.

"This is just an appetizer for me," he replied, laughing. "Anyone want some?"

"I have enough to eat, thank you," Gabby said.

"I'll pass. I don't like bellies. I only eat strips, but thanks anyway. They're all yours," Sage said.

"You don't know what you're missing," Cliff said, digging into his meal.

"Tomorrow morning I'm going to talk to Ms. Winters and see what she knows about Roger Perkin's disappearance," Sage said, drowning her fifties burger in ketchup.

"She may not remember very much. She is older now and it was a long time ago," Cliff said, dropping a huge clam in a dish of tartar sauce.

"You never forget your first love," Sage replied. "Maybe she knows something and doesn't realize it's important. It's worth a shot anyway."

"I knew you wouldn't let this go," Gabby said.

"What? He was murdered and someone is responsible for it. Besides, what's cooler than trying to solve a murder that took place more than forty years ago?"

"It will be hard to solve. People have died and

some have moved away who were in the area back then."

"That's what computers are for," Sage said. "I'm going to start by talking to my mom. She grew up here, too, and might remember something."

"She was only like ten or so. Do you really think she will remember anything about it?" Gabby asked.

"I don't know, but it's worth a shot. I haven't been to the shop for a couple of weeks and it's time I paid her a visit."

The conversation returned to the work which needed to be done at the farm to get ready for the autumn festivities. Apple picking was in full swing, and the crates Cliff had gone to pick up at the Perkins farm would have been put into use right away. Unfortunately, he had to leave without taking even one with him.

It was decided the friends would have a get together at Sage's house on Halloween night after their work at the hayride was done. Each couple would bring something for a potluck supper. Sage would provide the dessert in addition to a big crock pot of her famous beef stew. Gabby would bring some kind of appetizer, but she wasn't sure what yet. Cliff volunteered to bring a couple of gallons of freshly squeezed cider they could drink cold or heat up with cinnamon sticks and orange slices.

After lunch they went their separate ways. Cliff returned to work at the farm and Sage and Gabby went to Sage's workshop to unload what they managed to put in the van before the skeleton was discovered.

"Do you want to go to *This and That* with me?" Sage asked, setting the pile of barrel staves on a table in the storage trailer.

"I'd love to, but this is my only day off this week, and I need to go grocery shopping."

"Okay. Thanks for all your help this morning. I know you never planned on finding a skeleton like you did. Do you still want to not go back again when the sheriff says we can return?"

"I know I said I wouldn't go back but I will. Let me know when so I can arrange for a day off from the salon," Gabby answered, climbing into her car.

"I'll call you, and we can go on your next day off. I can take any time off I need to so we can work around your work schedule."

"Awesome. Talk to you then. Say hi to your mom for me."

Sage watched her best friend drive away and turned to lock up the trailer when she spotted some paper sticking out of a small vanity drawer they had taken from the barn. Opening the drawer, she found a leather-bound book which had been crammed in the drawer, open, so the pages were all disheveled and torn. She carefully removed the book, closed it and took it back to her shop.

Locking the handwritten journal in a safe hidden behind her tool rack until she could sit and look at it, she left for her mom's shop. Sage rolled down the van window letting the crisp autumn air blow on her face. Her long auburn hair blew around in the breeze occasionally landing in her mouth as she sang with the radio.

The parking lot at *This and That* was packed with cars and Sage had a hard time finding a spot to park. Figuring her mom was having some kind of sale and that accounted for all the extra shoppers, she parked out on the street and walked to the shop. It was empty. No customers, not even her mother was around. She heard muffled voices coming from the back of the shop and went to find out what was going on.

Folding chairs, arranged in a circle on the back patio were full of locals who Sage recognized. Sarah Fletcher looked up from her clipboard and spotted her daughter. She motioned she would join her inside.

"What's going on?" Sage asked, looking at her mom's red eyes.

"We're holding an emergency meeting of the selectmen and the town council members. Do you remember Ella White?"

"Sure, she's the sheriff's wife," Sage replied.

"She passed this afternoon at the hospital," Sarah said, sadly.

"Sheriff White must be devastated. She wasn't that old, was she?"

"Ella was only sixty-four. This was totally unexpected. We're having an emergency meeting to find a replacement for Gerald while he takes some time off to deal with the arrangements and some time to grieve. We have agreed Andy Bell should step in while Gerald is out."

"Andy will do a great job. With him in charge the sheriff won't have to worry about anything to do with work. You will let me know about the services, won't you?"

"I will. Did you come here for a reason or just visiting your old mom?" Sarah asked.

"I came for a reason, but it can wait. And just so you know, and you hear it directly from me, we found a skeleton in Marie Perkins' barn this morning. The sheriff thinks it may have been Roger Perkins because of a watch chain which was found in the pocket of the overalls that was in the chest around the bones. Marie identified it as one she gave her husband."

"Oh, dear. Did he die in the barn, and no one knew he was there? Everyone thought he ran off with his mistress."

"He was murdered. He was hit on the back of the head if the crack in his skull is any indicator and then stuffed in a chest at the back of the barn."

"Leave it up to you to find another body," Sarah said, shaking her head. "Poor Gerald. He's had a rough day for sure."

"Gabby found it and boy, did she freak out. I'll let you get back to your meeting. I'll come over tomorrow to talk to you about Roger and Lucy."

"It sounds like you've found a new mystery to solve and you're getting right into it."

"I have. I'd love to be able to figure out who the murder suspect is from over forty years ago."

"That person may have moved or even be dead by now," Sarah replied. "You may be chasing a ghost."

"It wouldn't be the first time I chased a ghost," Sage said, smiling, thinking back to their ghostly encounter at the lighthouse this past summer.

"Just be careful. It's been a secret for all these

years and the person who committed the murder may want it to stay that way," Sarah warned.

"I will and I'll see you tomorrow. I'll bring some cider donuts and you can provide the tea," Sage said, leaning in and kissing her mom on the cheek.

"When can I expect some more flipped items? My shelves are looking a little empty and there is plenty of floor space to fill."

"I'll bring a load over next week. I have to help Cliff set up the hayride this weekend," Sage said, heading for the front door. "Love you!"

"Love you more," her mother replied.

Sage arrived home and stood in her driveway looking at her workshop and her house. She had planned to take the whole day off and didn't want to start working on a project this late in the afternoon. A loud meow sounded from the window on the side of the house.

"I hear you, Motorboat. I'll be right there," she yelled.

Her two cats met her at the door. They rubbed up against her legs all the while meowing. She stepped forward to close the door and almost tripped over them.

"Come on, guys. Give me a break. At least let me in the house or I can't feed you."

It was almost like the cats understood the word feed and ran to their bowls, sitting and watching her. She opened a can of their favorite food and split it between the two. They hungrily dug into their food.

"Geez, guys. It's like you haven't eaten in a month and you just ate this morning," she said, laughing. "Now for the job at hand."

She headed for the back of the house and climbed the stairs leading to the attic. The space was well organized as Sage had taken the time last winter when it was too cold to work out in her workshop to sort and organize all her holiday items and childhood items stored there.

The back corner held all her Halloween decorations. Being Sage's favorite holiday, she had twice as many boxes for this holiday than all the others combined. She would take them downstairs, a couple at a time, pick what she wanted to use for that year, return the boxes to the attic and retrieve some more to go through.

"Well, hello, old friend," she said, standing in front of a life-sized vampire.

Next to the vampire stood a life-sized witch, mummy and werewolf. Sage always set them up on her porch to greet trick-or-treaters but had agreed to let Cliff use the figures this year for his hayride. They were all animated and could provide a scary factor when the guests rode by in the hay wagon. She brought them downstairs, one by one, so Cliff could load them in his truck that night when he came for supper.

The cats had finished eating and were now running around in the attic playing hide and attack with each other in amongst the piles of containers. Sage would go downstairs, and the cats would follow. A few times she had to shoo them out of the boxes as she sorted her decorations. Smokey found a furry spider in one box, grabbed it with his teeth and took off for the living room with it.

I'll get it back later.

Each room in the house had a theme. The kitchen was a witch's den with potion bottles, spider webs and several cauldrons. Each cauldron held different colored fluff simulating liquids with spiders crawling out of them. A full-sized broom sat next to the back door, ready to fly if necessary.

The dining room had always been Sage's favorite place to decorate. Skeletons sat in each chair, all posed in different positions with a fully loaded table in front of them. Black metal spider chandeliers with blood red candles were set at each end of the table over a black lace tablecloth. Plates full of bloody body parts were placed in front of each skeleton. Spider webs stretched from chandelier to chandelier and around the room.

Now if I can keep the cats down off the table, we'll be all set.

The living room had always been the candle and pumpkin room. Pumpkins of all colors, shapes and sizes were spread around the room. Candles were mixed in with the pumpkins to make pretty autumn displays versus the gruesome, scary displays in the other rooms. Sage had been collecting pumpkins since she was a little girl and every year her mother would add a new one to her already huge collection.

Sage looked at her watch and discovered she had been decorating for over five hours and Cliff was due at any time for supper which she hadn't even started to prepare yet.

"You two behave in here and don't get into any of my decorations," she warned the cats as she headed for the kitchen.

"Who's hungry?" Cliff asked, coming through the door with a large pizza box.

The cats ran to greet him as he placed the box on the kitchen table.

"This looks great," he said, looking around the kitchen.

"I'm glad you think so because I got so busy decorating, I forgot to start our supper."

"I'm glad I stopped for pizza. Are those the figures you are letting me use for the hayride?"

"They are. Do you think you can find a place for them in any of the scenes?"

"I already know where I am going to place them. They move, right?"

"They do, and the werewolf makes howling noises."

"Nice. The kids will love that," Cliff replied. "Let's eat while the pizza is still hot."

Sage grabbed a couple of plates out of the cabinet and two beers from the fridge. Just as they sat down to eat, a loud crash sounded from the living room. Smokey came flying by them from the area in question.

One of Sage's purple lace ceramic pumpkins was in a hundred pieces.

"Oh no," Sage said, walking forward to where the smashed pumpkin was sitting on the floor. "My mom gave me that one the first year I moved into the house. Maybe I shouldn't put out decorations this year and wait until the cats get a little older."

"Or maybe you could put away the really special

ones and leave the rest out to enjoy," Cliff said, returning with a broom and dustpan.

"I suppose," Sage sighed. "That was my favorite pumpkin. Smokey couldn't have broken one of the others. No, he had to choose my purple lace one to play with."

"I don't think he knows the difference," Cliff replied, sweeping up the broken pieces of ceramic pumpkin. "The way he took off, you might not have to worry about him getting near the others. The noise sure scared him."

"Good. Maybe he learned a lesson," Sage replied. "I should go make sure he is all right and the pumpkin didn't land on him."

"He looked like he was heading for the mud room. I'll finish up here while you go find him."

Sage found her furry roommate wedged in between the wall and the dryer. She coaxed him out by sitting on the floor and talking to him quietly. He curled up in her crossed legs until his little heartbeat slowed and he was calm again. She picked him up and brought him in to be with his brother who was lying on the couch.

"All good?"

"He's fine. The noise scared him but he's with

Motorboat on the couch. They'll both be asleep before too long. Now, how about some of that pizza?"

Cliff flipped open the box.

"Pepperoni, green pepper, and onion. Best pizza ever," he announced.

"Smells heavenly. How about after supper you help me put up some of the outdoor lights?"

"Wow! I not only provide supper, but I also have to work while I'm here too," Cliff said, joking.

"You're so put upon," Sage said, rolling her eyes.

"I am, aren't I?" he said, laughing and taking a big bite of pizza.

Between the two of them, they ate almost the entire pizza. Fresh beers in hand, they walked outside to discuss where the lights would go. Once they formed a plan, they returned to the house to get the lights and light-up pumpkins.

Cliff was up on the ladder stringing up purple and orange twinkling lights on the existing hooks left there from the Christmas lights the previous year. Sage was on the ground decorating the bushes on either side of the front porch.

A noise from the bushes lining her driveway caught her attention. As she got to her feet to see what was making the noise, a large rock hit the walkway right next to her.

CHAPTER THREE

"What was that?" Cliff asked from atop the ladder.

"Someone just threw a rock at me. And it has a note attached to it," Sage replied.

Cliff joined his girlfriend and together they opened the note.

On the paper in large red letters was a warning. LET IT GO.

"Let what go?" Sage mumbled.

"Someone probably got word the body was discovered at the Perkins' farm and you have been asking questions."

"That was quick, don't you think?"

"You know how gossip travels around this town, and it looks like someone wants the secret to stay a secret."

"No one threatens me and gets away with it. Now I am more determined than ever to find out what happened in the barn," Sage stated loudly. "Did you hear that, whoever you are that threw the rock? Now, get off my property before I call the police."

"I don't think they heard you. A motor just started up down the road. I believe they're already gone."

"Let's quit for the night. I'll finish up tomorrow," Sage suggested.

Cliff set the ladder down on the ground behind the workshop and they went inside. Sage grabbed two beers and they sat on the couch together trying to find something interesting on television. They couldn't find anything they wanted to watch so they turned it off.

"I'm going to talk to Lucy Winters in the morning. I want to get her side of the story, if she can remember back that far," Sage said.

"I don't know if I'm okay you're proceeding with this. Just be careful. The person throwing the rock may become more desperate if you get any closer to an answer."

"I know, but I also know people are going to put the blame on Marie Perkins and I feel deep down inside she had nothing to do with it," Sage replied.

"I agree. I'm going to head home. Six o'clock

comes early. I have to be out on the tractor collecting apples for the store bins before it opens. Some people don't want to pick their own and would rather buy them already picked."

"Did your mom make some of her famous cider donuts? I promised my mom I would bring some with me when I visit her tomorrow."

"There is a good stock of those already in the store. I'll see you then," Cliff said, kissing her and heading for the door. "Make sure you lock the house up after I leave."

"I promise and then I'm heading to bed, too."

Sage locked the door as soon as Cliff stepped down off the porch. She watched him walk to his truck through the small window in the door. As the truck drove away, she spotted a small glimmer of light in the bushes near her workshop. A person, dressed all in black, was crouching behind the biggest bush.

"I've called the police," she yelled, flinging the door open.

The figure took off running. Sage closed and relocked the door as she watched the person in black run down the driveway and disappear. The cats heard her yelling and sauntered into the kitchen to see what was happening. They sat at her feet looking up at her.

"That was a huge bluff, but it worked. Maybe I should get a dog. Then we all might feel a little safer," she said to the cats. "Who could that have been? It looked like a man when the figure was running away but I can't be sure."

Sage turned the porch light off and sat in the darkness of the mudroom watching out the window. Twenty minutes passed and she decided it was safe to go to bed.

"I'm going to check all the windows and doors before I go to bed."

Half an hour later, Sage was tucked in bed with the cats at her feet. She lay there, listening for any out of place noise but heard nothing. She eventually dozed off and slept through the night.

The next morning, she was in the kitchen starting her morning coffee. She glanced out the window as she was filling the carafe with water and saw the ladder Cliff had placed behind her workshop wasn't where he put it the previous night. She set down the carafe and walked out the back door.

Still not seeing the ladder she turned the corner toward the backyard. The ladder had been placed up against the house under one of the windows of her bedroom. Someone had been watching her while she slept. A shiver crept up her spine.

I guess it's time to get out my pepper spray and keep it on my bedstand at night.

She took the ladder down, collapsed it to its smallest size, and locked it in her workshop. Still kind of creeped out that someone had been watching her through the night, she returned to the kitchen locking the door behind her even though it was broad daylight out.

The cats got their breakfast while her coffee brewed. Sitting at the kitchen table, sipping her coffee, she had grabbed a pad of paper and pencil to comprise a list of names which could relate to the Perkins or Lucy Winters. The list wasn't very long as the murder happened before Sage was born and she didn't really have any idea who lived in Cupston back then. This would be one area her mom might be able to help with even though she herself was a young girl at the time.

Sage arrived at the Fulton Farm Store just as it opened. Cliff was filling the apple bins as she entered. She watched him work. His muscles bulged as he lifted the heavy apple crates and emptied them in the bins according to variety. She stood there smiling.

He is gorgeous and such a hard worker.

Cliff turned, experiencing the eerie feeling that

someone was watching him. He smiled when he saw who it was.

"Good morning! You're out and about early," he said, setting down the empty crate. "Going to see your mom?"

"I was hoping to get there early before she opened her shop so we could talk without being interrupted. I promised her cider donuts so here I am to collect them."

"They are over near the register area. The cashier will ring you out when you're done shopping. I have more apples to collect and have to get back out to the orchards. I'll see you later tonight?"

Sage stood there lost in thought. She was debating with herself on whether to tell her boyfriend about the ladder against the house and someone watching her while she slept. Deciding against it, figuring he would flip out; she kept the news to herself.

"Hello? Are you in there?"

"I'm sorry. Lost in thought," she replied, smiling.

"I know. Another mystery to solve," he said. "Are we on for supper?"

"Yes, we are and this time I promise to cook something for you."

"I got the results back early for the soil test we did on the back acres. They said that we could grow trees back there, but the soil had been somewhat depleted from all the constant years of growing corn."

"So, what are you going to do?"

"A suggestion was made to leave the area unplanted for a couple of years. Turn it over twice a year and let the soil replenish its nutrients before we plant rows of Christmas trees."

"Is that what you're going to do?"

"I think so. My dad wants to use the spreader to feed the soil once we turn it over to help it along. I think he's getting as excited about growing the trees as I am."

"I love your dad. He's always up for something new," Sage said.

"He is. There is never a boring moment with him around," Cliff said, proudly. "He went to the big Halloween store in Moosehead and bought a carload of decorations for the hayride. He's out there right now laying out the path for the hay wagon to take."

"I'll be here Friday afternoon to help set up. I'm looking forward to creating spooky scenes to scare the kids."

"I believe there will be about thirty people here to help. Once people found out we picked the 4H as the recipient this year volunteers started to sign up from all over the county. We could get the whole thing set up in one day."

"That would be awesome. Okay, you get back to work and I'm going to buy some donuts. I made room in my freezer this morning for a couple of dozen to get me through the winter," Sage said.

"I did one better. I bought a small secondhand chest freezer and filled it with donuts from the first batch my mom made."

"Maybe I'll just eat yours instead," she said, laughing. "I still have to bring my mom some as promised."

"You're lucky I like you. I don't usually share my stash of donuts with anyone, but for you I'll make an exception," Cliff said, kissing her on the cheek. "I'll see you at supper."

Sage watched him walk out the side door. Her mind went back to when she debated on even going out on a date with Cliff and now, she can't imagine a day going by without him in it.

"You got yourself a good one," Lillian the cashier stated.

"I do, don't I?" Sage replied, smiling.

"His mother and I wondered if he would ever find the right one. Although between you and me, he's had a secret crush on you for a while now. Don't you ever tell him I told you that," she said.

"Have you worked here long?" Sage asked, setting two bags of warm cider donuts on the counter.

"On and off since the farm was established. I'm Cliff's Aunt Lillian. His dad is my brother," she replied.

"I had no idea he had other family in the area."

"There's lots of us around. There was eight of us brothers and sisters all who had our own families and raised them here in Cupston."

"So, you have been here your whole life?" Sage asked, adding a gallon of fresh pressed cider to her pile.

"I have. I'm the second oldest of all the siblings," she answered. "I work here part time in the autumn when the farm is the busiest and it gets me out of the house to socialize."

"Does your husband work here, too?"

"My Buster died many years ago. My daughter and two granddaughters live in Moosehead where her husband's job is located. When I'm not working here, I volunteer at the historical society."

"That must be an interesting job," Sage said. "You must know a lot about the town's history and it's residents."

"My fair share, I guess. Cliff tells me you are looking into the murder that happened at Perkins' Farm. I see the gleam in your eye. What do you want to ask me?" she asked, smiling.

"Do you know Lucy Winters?"

"I do. Lucy was a year ahead of me in school."

"Were you close friends?"

"Not really. She did date my cousin Lenny for a while."

"Was that before or after she met Roger Perkins?"

"Long before that. Lucy didn't meet Roger until she had graduated from high school and was working as a telephone operator. I can't for the life of me remember who she was dating at that time though."

"But she was dating someone else when she started to see Roger?"

"She was."

"I wonder if this person found out she was going to run off with Roger and he took matters into his own hands to stop it from happening."

"You must remember. Back then, the story was they ran away together until Lucy returned by herself. Then the story changed to Roger couldn't take the town knowing about his affair and left on his own so Marie wouldn't face any further embarrassment than she already had. Or, maybe, Marie started the rumor after she took matters into her own hands."

"I don't think Marie killed her husband. She was as shocked as we all were when the skeleton was found."

"It was a long time ago and Marie could have forgotten she left him in the barn. Stories flew rampant around town, and nothing was ever proved one way or another, nor was Roger Perkins ever found."

"Were there many newspaper articles printed at the time when Roger Perkins disappeared?"

"Quite a few. Most were speculation on the part of the editors. If you like when I return to work on Monday, I can pull some of them up for you and print them out. There may be a clue somewhere in there which would help you in your search for a solution," Lillian offered.

"That would be wonderful, thank you."

"You know your mother used to hang around in the same group of friends as Lucy's youngest nephew, Phillip. She might remember something from back then."

"I'm heading there next. I promised her cider donuts, so I had to stop here first."

"Swing by the historical society after lunch time

on Monday. That will give me a few hours to find what you need. Your total is eleven-thirty-five."

Sage handed her a ten and a five with the instruction to put the change in the 4H container sitting on the counter next to the register. She climbed in her car, waved to Cliff who was returning with a full load of apples from the orchard, and drove toward *This and That*.

Her mother's car was the only vehicle sitting in the parking lot. It was still an hour before opening time, so the mother and daughter would have some time to sit on the front patio while enjoying their beverages and donuts.

"Hello! Anyone here?" Sage yelled, entering the front door.

"Back here," her mother replied.

"I brought donuts," Sage announced, holding up the white bag.

"Great! I am just about done setting up this display of new English China. Pretty, isn't it?"

"I love it. Too bad I already have a set as I love the different shades of purple in that one."

"You could always bring in your set and swap it out for this one if you like it that much," her mother suggested.

"Where did it come from?"

"Marie Perkins is down-sizing and she dropped off a bunch of stuff. She doesn't want to consign it, just gave it to me to sell for the shop's profit. It was kind of weird actually," Sarah said, crawling over a pile of boxes.

"What was weird?" Sage asked, extending a hand for her mom to grab to keep her from losing her balance.

"I tried to talk her into consigning the pieces, but she wanted nothing to do with it. She insisted she had plenty of money for a woman her age. She also said that none of this stuff was hers to begin with as it belonged to the previous owner and had been left in the barn."

"That means she must have received clearance from the sheriff's office to go back in there again if that's where all these things came from. What's so weird about that?"

"It was what she was doing as she unloaded the boxes that was weird," Sarah said, turning on the flame under the teakettle. "As I would set down a box on the floor, Marie perused through each one as if she was looking for something."

"Did you ask her what she was looking for and offer to help her find it?" Sage asked, taking down the teacups from the shelf behind the register.

"She got all flustered and told me if she saw it, she would know. I didn't push it anymore and finished emptying the rest of the truck."

"It's too bad she didn't tell you what it was she was searching for in case you came across it while unpacking the boxes. Especially if it was a small piece of jewelry like a ring or something."

Settling in on the front patio, Sage's cell phone signaled a message was left for her. Opening it up, Cliff had said he had received a call from Marie the barn was free again and he could come pick up all the apple crates he needed. She also mentioned he might want to bring Sage with him.

"I guess I'll be making a trip to the Perkins' farm this afternoon," Sage said, setting her phone on the table in front of her. "Have you heard from the sheriff? I hope he's doing okay."

"I spoke to Gerald this morning. He's hanging in there as well as to be expected. Ella's passing was so unexpected I don't think he's had time to process what has happened yet."

"I guess it just proves that tomorrow isn't promised."

"Gerald was only three years away from retiring and then he and Ella were going to travel. Such a shame really."

"If there's anything I can do to help for the service please let me know," Sage offered.

"I will. Now, what did you really come over here for? Information?"

"Boy, can't I visit my own mom without being under a cloud of suspicion?"

"No. I know how you work. Donuts for information. Am I right?"

"Yes, you are. I was going to ask you about Lucy Winters, but Lillian, Cliff's aunt, said you used to hang around a group of people that included Lucy's nephew, Phillip Winters."

"I haven't heard that name in many years, but, yes, Phillip was in my group of friends."

"Did you know him well?"

"Not really. We socialized in school, but he was a hired hand at the Perkins farm from age sixteen on. His family lost everything in a fire, so all the sons went to work early on to help the family replace all they lost. Roger Perkins gave all four brothers jobs working the fields and paid them well to get the family back on track."

"So that branch of the Winters family had no problem with Roger Perkins?"

"Not as far as I know. He helped them every way

he could including a loan to rebuild the house that burnt down."

"Is Phillip still in the area?"

"No, after college he moved to France and as far as I know he still lives there."

"What about Lucy? How well do you know her?" Sage asked, reaching for a second donut.

"My mother knew her more than I did as they were in school together. When the story broke around town that Lucy was leaving with Roger, I remember my mother being quite shocked as Lucy was such a loner and was never involved with anyone."

"Lillian said she couldn't remember if Lucy was dating anyone else at the time or not."

"I very much doubt she was, but I can't be sure. She never dated in school and went to work for the phone company as an operator right after she graduated. She worked the night shift, or the graveyard shift as they used to call it because there were fewer people around at that time of night."

"Do you think that's where she met Roger?"

"Could be. Then again, she might have met him while he was working with her brother's family to help them start again. I don't think anyone really knows now but Lucy."

"I wish Grandma was alive so I could talk to her about Lucy," Sage said, sighing.

"I wish she was, too. I miss my mother every time I pick up one of these teacups we are drinking from. They were hers; you know. She loved her tea."

"I think that gene was passed down to both of us," Sage replied, taking a sip of her hibiscus tea. "And if I remember correctly, Grandma always used honey in her tea, never sugar."

"True, she always had a gallon jar of honey on the counter next to the window above the sink. I called it the magical jar as it was always full no matter how much tea we drank," Sarah said, smiling. "It wasn't until years later that I found out our next-door neighbor had hives and he was the one keeping the jar full in exchange for your grandma's homemade pies at Thanksgiving. I swear she made pies for half the town around the holidays."

"They were tasty. Now, back to the matter at hand. Can you think of anyone back then who had a problem with Roger? For any reason?"

"No one comes to mind except for Parker Hawkes. Back then he got into financial trouble and the bank took away a big chunk of his land to pay back bank loans. Roger bought the land in an auction which didn't please Parker very much."

"Do you think he couldn't have killed Roger to get even?"

"No, impossible."

"Why?"

"Parker was killed in a plowing accident several years before Roger disappeared. As a matter of fact, Roger returned a large portion of the land to Parker's widow so her sons could work the land and the family could carry on and not have to move from Cupston."

"He doesn't sound like a person anyone could hate," Sage said, shaking her head.

"He was very well liked. It doesn't make sense that he would end up in a trunk, murdered," Sarah replied.

"Good morning, all!" Flora said, cheerfully, as she turned the corner from the back yard.

"Good morning," the two women replied in unison.

"What's the special occasion that we are having tea on the patio? And are those cider donuts?"

"They are. Straight from Fulton Farm. Help yourself," Sage answered, holding up the bag.

"Don't mind if I do," she replied, reaching into the bag.

"Do you remember Marie and Roger Perkins?" Sage asked.

"I only met Marie a few years ago and I never knew Roger. I didn't live in the area back then."

"Thanks anyway."

"Trying to figure out who killed him and stuffed him in the trunk?" Flora asked.

"I am."

"Have you talked to Lucy Winters?"

"I'm heading to the flowers shop as soon as I leave here," Sage replied.

"Lucy gets very defensive when Roger's name is brought up. You might want to ease into your discussion with her," Sarah advised.

"I have a real reason to go there. I am going to be ordering flowers for Ella's service. Mom, do you want me to sign the card from both of us?"

"That's sweet, but no thank you. I will be sending my own arrangement."

A car pulled into the parking lot.

"I'll go in and set up the register. It's almost opening time," Flora said.

"I'm going to head out, too."

"Not before I grab another donut," Flora, said, laughing and reaching for the bag.

"I'm leaving the bag here, you can have as many as you want," Sage replied.

"Wonderful! May I bring one to Paul when I go home for lunch?"

"Be my guest," Sage replied. "I'll talk to you later, Mom. Love you."

"Love you more," Sarah said, picking up the teacups and heading into the shop.

Sage rolled up her van window as it had started to rain as she sped along the back roads toward town. The holes on the dirt road were already filling with water and her van shuddered and groaned each time she hit a deeper hole disguised under the rainwater.

I don't know how much longer this old van of mine is going to last.

The Purple Petunia Flower Shop was located on Main Street at the south end of town. This early in the morning traffic should have been light going into town. The closer Sage got to Main Street the more the traffic was backed up and almost at a standstill.

She edged her way forward and finally saw what the problem was. An ambulance as well as two cruisers were parked in front of the flower shop.

CHAPTER FOUR

Sage swung into the first available parking space she could find and walked on foot to the flower shop. The rain had let up to a soft drizzle and a crowd had gathered around and was peering in through the front window. Sage walked closer to the open door in case one of the deputies came out and she could find out what was going on inside.

Andy Bell, the deputy filling in for the sheriff while he was on leave, spotted Sage and headed for the door. He waved her inside. As she entered, Sage noticed Lucy sitting in a chair in the corner of the room surrounded by paramedics.

"Is Lucy okay?"

"She's just shaken up. As she was unlocking the back door to come to work, someone rushed her from inside her office, knocked her down, and fled the scene."

"Did she see who it was?" Sage asked.

"No, she said he had on a ski mask and was dressed all in black."

"She knows it was he and not a she?"

"Lucy said he was very tall and extremely strong when he plowed her over."

"Was the motive robbery?"

"The office has been trashed. Whether the person was looking for money or something else is unknown. Lucy says it is well known she only leaves twenty-five dollars in the building at night which is to start the register off with the next day."

"It doesn't sound like a robbery. It sounds like this person was looking for something specific in the office. Why did you want me to come in here?"

"Lucy saw you through the window and asked to speak with you. She wouldn't say about what and insisted you would be the only one she talked to," Andy replied.

"Well, I guess I need to go see what she wants," Sage said.

"Shoo! Go away! I'm fine, I tell you!" Lucy said, refusing the medical help the paramedics were trying to provide for her.

"Lucy, I'm afraid there is nothing more we can do here. If you find what is missing from your office please give me a call. I'll dismiss the paramedics and the ambulance if you are sure you don't want to go to the hospital to be checked out," the deputy said, standing next to the elderly woman.

"Andy, I know you are just trying to do your job, but I insist I am fine. I need to speak to Sage, alone."

"Okay. I'll stop by later and check on you," Andy insisted.

"Whatever makes you feel better, young man," she said, dismissing the deputy with a wave of her hand.

"Let's pack it up, guys," he said to the paramedics and other deputies.

Lucy sat silent as she patiently waited for the men to leave her shop.

"I haven't got much time before the shop opens. You need to listen. I know who it was who broke into my shop this morning and why."

"Why didn't you tell Deputy Bell?" Sage asked, sitting down on the bench next to the elderly woman.

"How do you turn in your own family?" she asked sadly.

"What do you mean? You know he was a family member?"

"It was my nephew, Billy Winters. I recognized his aftershave."

"Why would your relative break into your shop? Why wouldn't he just ask you if you had what he was looking for?"

"Because what he is looking for could place his dad in the barn the same day Roger Perkins died."

"Are you saying there is some kind of evidence around after all these years which could prove who killed Roger?"

"Roger had a business journal he wrote everything in religiously every day. Meetings, expenditures, and the fields that were worked during that week. My brother, after finding out we were going to be leaving town that night insisted on visiting with Roger and having a man to man talk with him."

"Are you insinuating your brother could have killed Roger and left his body in the barn?"

"I don't know, but if my brother called Roger to meet with him his name would have surely been in the business journal. I think my nephew thought he was protecting his dad by finding and disposing of said journal," Lucy replied, wringing her hands. "I went to the hotel where Roger and I were to meet, and he never showed. I waited three days and never heard from him again. I couldn't get past the fact in my own mind that Roger was never seen again after his meeting with my brother."

"Did you ever ask your brother what happened that night?" Sage asked.

"I did, but he told me the situation was taken care of and I was not to ask about it again."

"And you never did? Ask about it, I mean."

"Back in those days, a woman didn't have a lot of say over her own life. My brothers were older, and I was raised not to argue with them as they were men and knew better than I. After the three days passed, I assumed Roger left without me. He no longer loved Marie and I figured he left to start a new life somewhere else without either of us. It broke my heart. I loved him so."

"Is that why you never married?"

"I always held on to the hope Roger would return to me and now I know why he never did; he was unable to."

"Do you think your brother was the last one to see Roger alive?"

"He was mad the day he left to talk to him. The fact that Roger Perkins made a fool out of his wife by carrying on an affair right under her nose, Perry felt like he was stringing me along and would do the same thing to me down the road. I tried to explain that would never happen, but he wouldn't listen to a single word I said before he stormed out of the house."

"Do you think he did something to Roger? Maybe out of anger or by accident?"

"I don't know. Until Roger's body was found I honestly thought he left town."

"If your brother didn't do it, can you think of anyone who might have?" Sage asked.

"Roger was loved by everybody."

"Even Marie?" Sage asked, watching the woman's reaction.

"Even Marie. We talked some months later and she forgave me for all that happened. If it wasn't for her and her kind words around town, I might not have been able to stay here. We became good friends after a few years."

"So where do you think this business journal is?"

"I would have to assume it is somewhere in the barn. Roger spent most of his time there and conducted almost all his meetings there. It was like his private inner sanctum."

"Who else would know about this journal?"

"Everyone in town knew about it. Roger took it everywhere with him."

"Why would your family assume you had the journal?"

"That afternoon, Roger dropped off two suitcases full of personal things he was taking with him when we left. Everything else he left for Marie. Maybe now that the body has been found and Roger was murdered, people assumed I still had the journal, but I don't. I never had it in my possession to begin with."

"Where are the two suitcases? Do you still have them?"

"I do. I couldn't bear to part with them."

"You need to check through them and see if the journal might be hidden in the lining or at the bottom under the other contents."

"You can check them yourself. They are up in the attic here at the shop. The stairs over in the corner will take you up there. The suitcases are in the back corner under a white sheet," Lucy said. "I haven't touched them since the day I first put them up there."

"I'll be right back," Sage said, hurrying toward the stairs.

Several minutes later she returned with two leather satchels. Sage set them on the floor in front of Lucy and waited.

"Go ahead and open them," Lucy said.

She picked up the first of the two and set it on the bench between herself and the elderly woman. The lock opened easily, and Sage peered inside. The top layer of contents were clothes belonging to Roger Perkins.

"May I take things out?" Sage asked.

"Please do," Lucy said, reaching for the clothes Sage had set down on the bench and held them up to her face. "I can still smell him after all these years."

After all the clothes had been emptied, Sage picked up the satchel which still had some weight to it. She set it down and started to check the satin lining inch by inch. On one end she found some hand stitching that didn't belong there.

"Do you have some scissors?"

"On the worktable. Did you find something?"

"Someone took the time to stitch the lining back together on one end. With your permission I'd like to open it up and see if anything is underneath."

"I don't think it will be the journal. Why would he have to hide it?" Lucy asked.

Sage carefully snipped the snitches that held the hole closed. She reached in and pulled out a brown parcel tied with twine. A second and third followed.

"That's it," Sage said, turning the lining inside out.

"I wonder what's inside that could have been so important that he had to hide it?" Lucy said.

"Why don't you open one of them?" Sage suggested.

The woman's hands trembled as she tried to undo the twine knot.

"Would you like some help?" Sage offered.

"Please. I can't make these old hands work right now."

Sage was able to release the knot and handed the package back to Lucy. The brown paper was delicate and started to fall apart as she unfolded it. Both women gasped when the contents were exposed. Stacks of old money in bands of one-thousand dollars each fell to the floor.

"Roger said we would never hurt for money when we started our new life together. This must have been what he was talking about," Lucy whispered.

Sage picked up the money on the floor and watched while Lucy opened the remaining two parcels. Each was filled with money banded in the same fashion as the first.

"I wonder if this is what Marie is looking for," Sage mumbled under her breath.

"All these years and I never knew this was up in the attic," Lucy said.

"There must be over twenty-thousand dollars here. That was a good amount of money back then.

Roger must have really loved you to want to provide such a good life for you."

"What am I going to do with it?" Lucy asked.

Sage glanced over Lucy's shoulder and saw a figure outside peering through the window.

"Stay put," she said, running for the back door.

She flung open the door and ran outside, but she was too late. The person was gone. Locking the back door behind her, she returned to Lucy who was looking at her waiting for an explanation.

"Someone was watching through the window. They had to have seen the money as it fell on the floor," Sage explained.

"What am I going to do? One break-in is bad enough but now I have all this money. Help me, please."

"The first thing we are going to do is remain closed until Deputy Bell can get back here. He will escort you to the bank where you will open a safety deposit box to put this money into for safe keeping."

"I already have a box. Can I just use that one?"

"Of course, you can. It is better not to keep it here now that someone else knows about it. Let me call Andy."

.While the women waited for him to arrive, they checked the second satchel. It contained more clothes, some personal papers including life insurance policies; one each in the name of Marie and Lucy.

At the bottom Sage found a blue velvet ring box. She pulled it out and Lucy teared up looking at it.

"My ring," she whispered. "Roger showed me the box but never showed me the ring inside. He said I would see it when we were settled in our new life, and he could officially put the ring on my finger."

"Open it," Sage said.

"Do I dare?" she asked, gasping.

"It was supposed to be your engagement ring, right? Aren't you curious what it looks like?"

"I am, I thought it was long gone," she replied, grasping the cover of the box and flipping it open.

Inside, seated on a cushion of white satin was the most exquisite ring Sage had ever seen. A center stone, consisting of a brilliant emerald cut diamond, surrounded on both sides by a pear-shaped, dark blue matching sapphires was set in a platinum setting.

"It's gorgeous," Sage whispered.

"Is it really mine to keep? Can I wear it now?"

"I would say yes, but let's check with Andy and see what he thinks. He might suggest you put it in the safety deposit box with the money until we catch who broke in and figure out who killed Roger Perkins."

"That would be the smart thing to do, I guess," she said, closing the ring box.

Deputy Bell knocked on the front door.

"I'll get it," Sage said, going to the front door and unlocking it.

"Are you okay, Lucy? Did you change your mind about going to the hospital to be checked out?" the deputy asked.

"No, I'm still fine. But I have another problem now," she said, holding up some of the money.

"Whoa! Where did that come from?" Bell asked.

Sage explained where the money came from, and that Andy's help was needed to get it to the bank and safely secured as someone had been looking through the back window and knew it was in Lucy's possession. Deputy Bell agreed.

"What about my ring?" Lucy asked.

"Personally, I don't see any reason you can't wear it right now if you chose to. Just be careful about flashing it around to people you don't know," Andy suggested.

"For over forty years I waited to see this ring and now I can wear it. My Roger really did love me in spite of what was said," Lucy said, slipping the ring on her finger. "Oh, dear, it seems I have lost weight since then. Maybe I better put it away until I can get it sized so it doesn't fall off my finger and I lose it."

"I think that's the smart thing to do," Sage agreed.

"Grab your coat, Lucy. The quicker we get this to the bank the better I will feel about you here in the shop by yourself," the deputy stated. "And I assume you are already busy with all the flowers being ordered for Ella's funeral service."

"It's already started. Ella was a much-loved person and so is Sheriff White. I do have Annie coming in to help me fill all the orders for the service on Saturday."

"That makes me feel better you won't be here by yourself," Andy replied.

"I won't and Cliff Fulton has offered the use of his truck to move all the arrangements to the funeral home," Lucy said. "Shall we go?

"After you," Andy said, waiting at the door while Sage repacked the money into the satchel leaving the clothes on the bench so it wouldn't be too heavy for the elderly lady.

"Thank you, Sage, for everything today."

"I'll be back. I need to order flowers for Ella's service which is why I came in here today."

A customer knocked on the door.

"Maybe you had better put up a sign on the door

that you will be back in an hour," the deputy suggested. "I'll escort you to and from the bank and by then Annie should be here."

"She's due at eleven. There's a return at this hour sign under the counter at the register. Be a dear, Sage, and hang it on the door for me and set the return time at an hour from now."

Sage did as she was asked and explained to the customer waiting at the door they would have to come back in an hour. As Lucy was locking the door, Sage stood guard. The deputy helped Lucy into the front seat of the cruiser and set the satchel in her lap. Sage looked around to see if anyone was watching what was happening as Lucy was escorted off in the cruiser. She thought she might be able to spot the person peering through the window earlier, but no one was around that seemed interested.

"Hello," Sage said, answering her cell phone.

"Where are you? I'm going up to Marie's place and wanted to know if you were coming with me," Cliff said.

"I'll meet you there. Are you going right now?"

"I'm leaving the farm now so I should be there in about twenty minutes," Cliff replied.

"I should get there about the same time. I'll see you then," she answered, hanging up the phone.

Sage drove along, rehashing the information she had gleaned from Lucy making a mental note to be on the lookout for the business journal which belonged to Roger as they dug through the piles in the barn. If Roger was killed in there then it only seemed plausible the journal had to be somewhere near where the body would have been. Unless someone had taken it that night.

"Hey, beautiful," Cliff said as she exited her van.

"Hey, yourself," she replied, smiling.

"I've already loaded the crates that were outside the door. Want to help start another pile for me to load?"

"Shhhh! Did you hear that? Someone's inside the barn," Sage said, heading for the door.

The door was ajar.

"I'll go first," Cliff whispered, stepping in front of his girlfriend.

Cliff flung the door open, and light flooded the front section of the barn.

"Who's in here?" he demanded.

"Cliff! Don't scream like that! You could scare a person to death," Marie said, coming out from behind a pile of boxes.

"I'm sorry, Marie. Lucy's store was broken into

last night and we didn't know if the same thing was happening here," Cliff replied.

"Is Lucy okay?" Marie asked, stepping forward.

"She's fine. Why would someone break into her shop? It is a well-known fact she keeps no money there overnight. How strange."

You'll have to discuss it with her," Sage replied. "Can we help you look for something?"

"Uh, no, thank you. I was looking for some more smaller items to take to *This and That*."

"Are you sure? My mom said you were searching each box as she unloaded them at the shop as if you were looking for something specific."

"Fine, I was looking for Roger's business journal. Are you happy?"

"What could be in the journal that would make a difference over forty years later?" Sage asked. "Unless it contains the name of the killer."

"The week before Roger disappeared he withdrew a large amount of money from our joint bank accounts. I never found the money and was hoping maybe he mentioned what he did with it in the journal. All these years I assumed he took the money with him when he left, but now that I know he never left the farm, I thought the money might be hidden around here somewhere," Marie replied, sitting down.

"You could have told my mom what you were looking for. If she found it I'm sure she wouldn't have kept it," Sage said.

"I don't think she would have either. It's a lot of money and sometimes it does funny things to people. I don't want treasure hunters converging on the farm thinking they might find it," Marie replied. "I'm going inside to lie down. Rummaging through this stuff has exhausted me. If you find the journal or the money, please keep it to yourself but tell me of course."

"I wonder what she'll do when she finds out Lucy Winters has the money?" Sage whispered as they watched Marie walk toward the house.

"Lucy has the money?" Cliff asked.

"She does. We found it this morning in Roger's satchel that he left with Lucy the day they were supposed to leave together. It's been sitting up in the flower shop attic all these years. Lucy had no idea the money was there. I'd still like to find Roger's business journal though."

"I have to get back to the farm soon. If you help me with the crates, I'll come back tomorrow and help you load what you need to take."

"I know where there is a good amount of them inside as I saw them in the short time I spent here yesterday. I'll bring them out and you can load them into your truck. Sound good?"

"Awesome!" he said. "We make a great team."

"Yes, we do. And I have a favor to ask. Keep your eyes open for the leather-bound journal as we go through stuff inside. It may be the key to all the answers we need."

She proceeded to tell Cliff about the break-in at Lucy's shop and the fact Lucy thought it was her nephew looking for the appointment book to protect his father. They chatted about what the journal could hold as they filled Cliff's truck with apple crates for the farm.

"That went quickly," Cliff said, slamming the tail-gate on the truck shut. "Are you heading home now?"

"I have to go back and place my order for flowers for Ella's service. It kind of got pushed to the side with everything else that happened," Sage replied. "I'm going to load a few things in the van, check on Marie, and then head to the flower shop."

"I won't be there for supper tonight. Dad and I have a meeting with the soil conservation agent to see if we can formulate a plan for the back acres."

"That's exciting. Maybe you'll be planting Christmas trees quicker than you think," Sage said, smiling. "I guess I will see you tomorrow then."

"Please be careful. We still don't know who threw the rock at you or who killed Roger. It could be anyone."

"I will. I'll lock the doors as soon as I get home," she said.

Cliff drove away with his load of apple crates. Sage grabbed the flashlight out of her van and went into the barn. She pondered over where the journal could have ended up if Roger had been hit from behind and dropped on the spot. The area around the chests would be a good place to start looking.

The chest which held the body had been taken by the medical examiner. Sage searched the entire area around the remaining chests and found nothing. She ran the conversation the day the body was found through her mind. The one thing she kept going back to was the gold chain found in the pocket of the overalls.

"The chain was there but what happened to the watch?" Sage mumbled out loud.

"I was wondering the same thing myself. As I said, Roger never went anywhere without it," Marie said, coming up behind her. "Do you think whoever killed him took the watch? It was solid gold and would have fetched a good amount of money back then."

"Could be, I don't know."

"I'm going to see Lucy to order flowers for Ella's service. Please lock up the barn when you're done," Marie requested, walking to the door.

I wonder if Marie has the watch hidden somewhere in the house.

"And no, I don't have the watch if that is what you are thinking," she said, exiting the barn.

Sage found a pile of heating grates that must have come out of an old house years ago and loaded them into the van to turn them into side tables. She made a mental note of the larger furniture pieces she would have Cliff help her with the following day. Old windows were loaded into the van which had many uses in Sage's line of work. Wooden shutters which she would turn into room dividers made their way into the van next.

Cases of empty wine bottles, all colors and sizes that would make gorgeous hanging lamps when she was done with them were stacked on the front passenger's seat. Boxes of hardware, drawer pulls, and lamp harps finished off the load.

"This place is a goldmine," Sage said, locking the door of the barn. "I'll be able to fill my whole storage trailer and have plenty to work on over the winter until the yard sales and estate sales start up again next spring."

It was getting late in the day and Sage wanted to make sure she got her flower order in for the funeral service. She decided to empty the van in the morning and went directly to the flower shop from the farm.

The place was busy as many customers were placing orders for Ella's service. Sage wandered around waiting for the line to go down so she could place her order. The locals joked with Lucy as forms were filled out and signed. Sage watched the elderly woman interact with her customers. Even Marie, who was there to order flowers, was very chummy with her long-ago competition.

It seems her actions as a mistress from years ago have all been forgotten. I guess everyone is entitled to a mistake.

Sage ordered a simple but nice arrangement of white roses, white mums, and white lilies. She signed the card and left the shop. Once at home she locked the doors and started her supper. The cats drove her crazy until they were fed and then they settled on the bay window ledge to clean themselves.

As she stood at the stove, mindlessly stirring her tomato soup, there was a loud thud from the living room and the cats came flying by her in a panic heading for the mudroom. She looked around the room and couldn't see anything out of place. She had that funny feeling of being watched and looked at the bay window where the cats had been lying. Someone was looking back.

CHAPTER FIVE

Sage pulled her phone out of her back pocket and dialed 911 while at the same time running for a bat standing in the corner of the room. The masked person realized he had been spotted and took off into the night. Minutes later, a cruiser came screaming into her driveway. Feeling safe with the deputy there, she exited her house with a flashlight in hand.

"Sage, are you okay?" Deputy Plummer asked.

"I'm okay, just a little shaken up, that's all."

"Someone was looking in your window?"

"Yes, someone wearing a black ski mask. He was standing over here," she said, leading the deputy to the bay window. "There are his footprints. It looks like he was wearing some kind of boots."

"Why would someone be looking in your window?" he asked.

Sage told him about the rock throwing incident and the same night the ladder being up against the back of her house while she slept.

"So, you think this has to do with the fact you are poking around trying to solve who killed Roger Perkins?"

"I believe so. Someone who is still in the area knows who murdered him and they don't want me finding out. This person might even be the murderer themselves or at the very least related to him."

"I don't think they'll come back tonight now that they were spotted," Deputy Plummer stated. "I'll have a cruiser swing by every hour or so and check on the place for any unusual activity. Do you want me to call Cliff?"

"No, he's at a very important meeting tonight and besides, I haven't told him about the ladder incident," Sage replied.

"You really need to tell him."

"I know, but I also know he will worry about me every second of the day. He has a lot on his plate right now with the farm and he doesn't need to be distracted. Especially now that Ella's service is on

Saturday which is the first day volunteers were supposed to be at the farm setting up the hayride."

"I forgot about that."

"Everyone will be attending including myself, Cliff and his parents. The service is at eleven with a get together afterwards. It doesn't look like we'll get back to the farm until at least two in the afternoon."

"The hayride doesn't open until Tuesday night. I think that will leave plenty of time to get it set up," Plummer stated.

"I hope so."

"Are you sure you're okay? I'll stay right here until you get in the house and lock the door."

"I'll be fine. I have a bat in every room of the house, and I rigged my own homemade alarms on the windows upstairs so I will be aware of anyone trying to get in," she replied.

"Head in the house. I'll see you at the service on Saturday."

"Good night, Dan. Thanks for everything," Sage said, walking up the steps to her house.

A terrible burnt smell was coming from the kitchen.

"My soup!" she said, running for the stove.

The red tomato soup had turned into a black, burnt-on mess at the bottom of the pan. Sage turned off the gas and set the pan in the sink. The water sizzled as it hit the hot metal.

"That's going to have to soak overnight," she mumbled. "I guess I can make a quick salad."

While sitting at the kitchen table eating her salad, her cell phone rang. Cliff had finished his meeting and was extremely excited about the results of the evening. After going over several programs to build up the nutrients in the soil, one was chosen that would allow the first trees to be planted in eighteen months.

"That's wonderful," Sage replied.

"I had another reason for calling. I wanted to know if you had some time tomorrow to help me transport some of the arrangements from Lucy's shop to the church. I wanted to put them in the back of the truck but I'm afraid the wind will be too much on the ride over. I was hoping we could pick up a load in your van at Marie's, empty it at your house, and then load your van with the arrangements. It's closed in and the wind won't do any damage to them."

"If you want to be at my house around nine, I'll have the coffee ready. We could be at the flower shop by noon to pick up the first load," Sage replied.

"Sounds like a plan. I'll see you then," Cliff said and hung up.

An hour later, Sage was in bed accompanied by her two cats.

The coffee had just finished brewing when Cliff pulled up in his truck. Sage had been up early emptying all the items into her shop she had loaded into the van the previous day. They returned to the kitchen together and Sage filled two travel mugs with steaming hot coffee to take with them on their morning trek to Marie's farm. The cats were racing around the house batting several of the fuzzy spiders they had dragged down off the dining room table.

"Your roommates like the Halloween decorations," Cliff said, laughing at Motorboat who was on his back holding a spider in his front paws and kicking at it with his back paws.

"I figured if I left the spiders to them, they wouldn't bother the rest of the decorations and so far it has worked," Sage replied. "Although, Smokey did get tangled up in some of the spider webs and didn't like it at all."

"Are you ready?" Cliff asked, opening the back door.

"Let me make sure my workshop is locked before we leave," Sage said, locking the door to her house.

On the way to the farm Sage decided to tell Cliff about the ladder incident. He was not happy that she hadn't said anything to him up until then and she apologized several times for not telling him.

"We are in a relationship. We're supposed to look out for each other," Cliff said, frowning. "Not keep secrets from each other."

The next few minutes of the ride passed in silence. Sage could tell Cliff was mad and she didn't know what to say to assure him it wouldn't happen again.

"Why is this person so interested in you? It can't be just because you are looking into the murder," Cliff said, finally breaking the silence.

"I don't know," she replied, sighing. "These people are actually giving me reasons to check into them instead of just staying silent and not drawing attention to themselves."

"I think the best thing we could accomplish is to find the journal and see what the last entries were."

The couple arrived at the barn. Cliff backed the van as close as he could to the door so they wouldn't have to carry the big pieces of furniture too far. Marie's truck was parked to the side of the door and had been loaded with boxes and smaller articles which Sage assumed was going to *This and That*.

"Marie is going to keep you and your mom in business for quite a while," Cliff said.

"She is. This barn is loaded with projects for my flipping business. I'll be able to fill my whole storage trailer with items to flip and sell."

"Let's get to work. What do you want to load first?"

Bureaus, shelving units and two dining room sets were loaded into the van. Sage found four old school desks at the back of the barn and took those with her to flip into bars for a smaller apartment. Smaller items like lamps, old plant stands, and folding chairs were set into the spaces that were not filled.

"I think we're done," Cliff said, looking into the van.

Marie exited her house, walked to her truck with her keys in hand.

"It looks like you are making headway in there. Still no sign of the journal, huh?"

"Not yet," Sage replied.

"I would really like to know what happened to Roger. Yes, he was leaving me, but he didn't deserve what happened to him. Sometimes love just fades away when you're so busy with life that you don't notice until it's too late."

"Did you still love Roger even after you found out he was having an affair with Lucy?" Sage asked.

"I did and told him so," Marie replied, not minding the personal questions being asked of her.

"When did you tell him?" Sage asked.

"The week before he left, or at least when I thought he left. I never did quite understand why he didn't take Lucy. That was a strange twist."

"Very strange," Cliff agreed.

"I'm off to see your mother. I love visiting Sarah and poking around her shop. Not that I need anything at this stage in my life, but it's always fun to browse. And Cliff, I did get a hold of your attorney friend and he was everything you said he was. Thank you for the recommendation."

"Great! Maybe he will remove some of the fear that your farm will end up in a developer's hands," Cliff said. "I'm glad I could help."

"Say hi to my mom for me," Sage said as Marie climbed up into her truck.

"I will. We'll see you tomorrow at Ella's service," she said, waving out the truck window as she drove away.

Cliff drove past Sage's house and parked in front of the trailer at the back of her property. It didn't take long to unload the van as it was mostly large pieces of furniture. As Sage was locking the padlock she heard a familiar meow coming from the far side of the trailer. Smokey came strolling out and headed straight for her meowing the whole time.

"How did you get out here?" she wondered, picking up the cat. "And where is your brother?"

"Is that Smokey?"

"It is. We need to get to the house right now," Sage said, hugging the cat tightly and breaking into a run.

"The slider is open," Sage said. "I'm really worried about Motorboat."

"Did you leave the slider open before we left?" Cliff asked. "Here Motorboat. Where are you?"

"No, I haven't had the slider open for several days. Someone must have broken into the house," Sage answered. "Motorboat! Come see me! Smokey, where is your brother?"

"You stay out here while I check to make sure no one is still in the house," Cliff said.

Sage held on to Smokey talking to him the whole time Cliff was inside. He returned to the slider with Motorboat in his arms.

"No one is here but I found this one in the mudroom. I guess he didn't want to venture outside like his brother did," Cliff said, holding the cat who had snuggled down into his arms.

"Let's get Smokey inside and close the slider," Sage said.

"You might want to call the station. Someone was looking for something and trashed your house," Cliff warned her as she stepped inside.

"You have got to be kidding? What could they possibly be looking for?" Sage said, looking at the mess around her and pulling out her cell phone.

"You really need to get an alarm system installed," Cliff suggested.

"Now that I have the cats, I might just do that to protect them. I wonder how the intruder got in."

"The window in the mudroom has been jimmied open. It's on the back of the house so no one would see the person breaking in in broad daylight."

"I haven't bought anything new that has any value. It has to be connected to the murder. The items from the barn are the only things I have brought to my house."

"Could it be possible that someone thinks you might have Roger Perkins' journal and came looking for it?" Cliff asked.

"It could be, I guess. Andy just pulled into the driveway. Let's go talk to him."

Twenty minutes later the deputy was leaving. There wasn't much he could do about the break-in, but he did offer to dust for fingerprints which Sage turned down. She wasn't even sure if anything was missing from the house.

Cliff wedged a piece of wood in the frame of the mudroom window to keep it from being opened again. Sage made sure the cats were settled in and gave them some kitty treats before the couple left for the flower shop.

The van was pulled up to the back loading dock. Lucy had already set over a dozen arrangements on the dock ready to be loaded and transported. The couple entered through the back door to find the flower shop owner. She was sitting at her desk, looking down into her lap. There were tears in her eyes. Lucy looked up, noticed the couple looking at her, and shoved something in the drawer of the desk.

"Lucy, are you okay?" Cliff asked her.

"It's been a long morning."

"I'm sorry. Is Annie here helping you?" Sage asked.

"She's been an angel through all this. There are fifteen arrangements out on the loading dock and fourteen more in the walk-in refrigerator. We still have eight more to finish. This is the busiest this shop has ever been."

"We can take one load over to the church and

come back for the rest. Do you think the others will be finished by the time we get back?" Sage asked.

"They should be. I'm not as quick as I used to be, but Annie is a firecracker," Lucy replied.

"Okay. We're going to load the flowers and we'll be back in a while," Cliff said.

"Did you happen to see what Lucy crammed in the drawer?" Sage asked Cliff as they loaded the flowers.

"No, I didn't. Why?"

"I saw a flash of something metallic before she dropped the item in the drawer. Why was she crying and so sad?"

"I didn't see what you did and there could be a million reasons she is sad and crying," Cliff replied. "Maybe she is upset about Ella dying. This is the first death of a local we have had in this town for a very long time."

"True. You're probably right. I'm going to tell Lucy we are leaving."

Lucy had returned to her worktable and was working on a large blanket arrangement with Annie. It was done in white roses, purple roses, assorted greens, and baby's breath.

"That is stunning," Sage said.

"It's from the sheriff," was all Lucy could say.

"I came in to tell you we are leaving with the first load and will be back in a bit," Sage said.

"We should be done with everything by the time you return," Annie stated, her hands busy weaving purple roses into the rows of white roses. "Thank you for stepping up and helping us. I usually deliver the arrangements in my car, but we have never had so many at the same time."

"Glad to help," Sage replied.

By mid-afternoon all the flowers had been delivered to the church. Cliff returned to the farm to get some work done there and Sage was at home cleaning up the mess in her house the intruder had made. While cleaning the kitchen she took out two good-sized steaks for her and Cliff for supper.

The cats were under-foot no matter where Sage was working. They followed her from room to room, talking to her like they were glad to have her at home. The papers covering her desk in the living room had been pushed to the floor and were everywhere. She picked them up a handful at a time when she noticed a slip of paper with her name and address on it.

This isn't mine. The intruder must have dropped it.

She ran to the kitchen and grabbed a plastic bag to put the paper in so it could be checked for finger-prints. Once it was safely tucked in the bag, she started to look for any other item the intruder could have dropped in his search.

"Hello!" Cliff yelled from the kitchen.

"Check this out," Sage said as he entered the living room.

"Why do you have a paper with your name and address on it?" he asked.

"I believe it was dropped by the person who broke in. If he needed my name and address it means he didn't know where I lived and maybe he didn't even know me," Sage replied.

"You think he was hired by someone who does know you?"

"I think so."

"Interesting. But who?" Cliff asked, picking up some of the pumpkins that had been dumped on the floor in the hasty search by the intruder.

"I don't know, but I would have to lean toward the same person who broke into the flower shop."

"Could be. He didn't find the journal there and maybe came here looking for it," Cliff replied.

"I think it's time Lucy tells Deputy Bell she thinks the person was her nephew. She didn't want to get him in trouble, and I kept my mouth shut because it was her decision to make. But now they have broken into my house and Lucy needs to fess up and tell Andy everything."

"I brought some fresh vegetables from the farm for supper," Cliff said, his stomach growling.

"I can take a hint. Let's go fix supper," Sage said, laughing.

While Cliff cooked the steaks on the grill, Sage prepared a nice salad and a big pan of summer squash with butter, salt and pepper. The cats were fed, and the couple sat down to eat supper. One bite in, Sage jumped out of her chair.

"I've had it all along," she said, running for the back door.

CHAPTER SIX

"Hey! Wait for me," Cliff yelled.

Sage grabbed her key ring off the hook at the back kitchen door. She ran to her workshop and fumbled with the key as she tried to get the door open. Once inside, she headed straight to the safe hidden behind her workbench.

"This is what everyone is searching for, and I had it all along," she said, pulling a tattered leather journal out for Cliff to see.

"It's been here the whole time and you didn't remember you had it?" Cliff asked.

"It was in one of the pieces of furniture I took from the barn the first day when the skeleton was found. In all the excitement I shoved it in the safe to look at it later and then forgot about it," she replied, opening the book to the front page. "Yes, it is Roger Perkins' business journal."

"Let's take it inside," Cliff suggested. "Just in case someone is watching the house."

They sat at the kitchen table eating and flipping through the worn journal.

"Some of the pages are gone," Sage stated.

"The only ones we really need to see are the ones from the last week he was alive," Cliff replied.

"True," Sage said, flipping to the end of the book. "Look, here's an entry for when he went to the bank and withdrew the money to take with him and Lucy. It looks like it was almost two weeks before he was going to leave."

"Well, we know where he kept the money," Cliff replied.

"He had appointments with his attorney, the local jeweler, and personal business meetings. He probably picked up Lucy's ring at the jewelers.

"I think we need to pay attention to the personal meetings he had. One of those people might be the killer," Cliff suggested.

"This is the last entry. It mentions a meeting with someone named Bryant. Do you know who that could be?" Sage asked.

"I have no idea," Cliff replied.

"I think we're getting closer to solving the murder. It's going to be a tough day for everyone in town tomorrow and I don't want to cause any kind of scene at the service," Sage said. "I think we should keep this to ourselves until the day after the service."

Cliff's cell phone rang. He talked briefly and hung up.

"That was Lucy. She had some last-minute flower orders, two of which are too big to fit in Annie's car. She was wondering if we could come by early in the morning before the service and take them to the church for her. I told her we would."

"I thought you'd be going with your parents," Sage replied.

"I was but I guess it's you and me now. Are you okay with that? What about your mom? Were you going to go with her?"

"No, she going over early to set up the banquet room downstairs for the get together after the service. I can help with the flowers."

"I can pick you up at nine which will give us plenty of time to deliver the flowers before people start arriving for the service," Cliff said.

"There's really not much more we can do with the journal until we find out who this Bryant person is.

Now the problem is where do I hide it so it will be safe," Sage said, looking around.

"Why don't I tuck it under my coat when I leave and take it to the farm? I can put it in the safe there and no one will be the wiser," Cliff suggested.

"I don't know if I want to involve your family in this. What if someone breaks into the farm and one of your parents get hurt?"

"Any other suggestions?"

"The journal has been safe out in my workshop. If you hide the book like you said we can walk out to the shop and return it to the safe behind my workbench. If you look out of the window to make sure no one is looking in, I can keep an eye on the door. I'll bring in something from the shop to the house to make it look like we went out there for a different reason."

"Okay. I'll grab two beers from the fridge and while I am behind the door I will slide the book in my waistband. We can walk out to the shop and hide the journal and come back in and finish eating."

"Sounds like a plan," Sage replied.

The couple walked out to the shop holding hands and laughing like they didn't have a care in the world. Once inside, Sage secured the journal in the safe while Cliff stood lookout. They carried a wooden crate of light fixture parts back into the house and placed it on the table. They finished their supper while Sage pretended to go through the box looking for what she needed. If anyone was watching it looked like a normal night in the life of a flipper.

Supper and the dishes done; Cliff left for home. Sage walked around the house to make sure all the windows and doors were locked and turned the lights out to go upstairs. It had been a long day and once her head hit the pillow she fell into a deep sleep.

"What am I going to wear?" she asked the cats, holding up several dresses. "I don't have anything all black and I don't want to wear anything too bright or flowery."

She settled on a black A-line skirt with a burnt orange cowl neck sweater. Black flats completed her outfit. Her hair was pinned into an updo with curly strands of hair lining her face.

"This is suitable," she said, looking in the full-length mirror on the back of her bedroom door. "It's almost nine. Come on, boys, let's go downstairs."

Sage was standing in the kitchen when Cliff pulled up and got out of his truck. She had never seen him dressed in a suit and not in jeans or overalls. He was wearing a black pinstripe, three-piece suit with a white dress shirt and a black tie. Her heart beat a little faster and she felt butterflies in her stomach as she watched him walk toward the house.

"Well, aren't you the handsome one?" Sage said, putting her arms around his waist.

"And look at you. I don't think I have ever seen you in make-up," he replied. "You're gorgeous."

"I don't have much reason to wear it in my line of work," she said, laughing.

"Is the house locked up?"

"Not yet. I'll grab my purse and we can go."

A quick stop at the flower shop and they were on their way to the church. They brought the arrangements inside and then went downstairs to see if Sage's mom needed any help with the food.

"Hi, Mom," Sage said, kissing her on the cheek. "What can we do to help?"

"Everything is ready to go. Shirley, Flora and I have been here since early this morning setting things up and I think we are done."

Sage took a look around the room. It was beautiful and simple. The tables were dressed in white tablecloths with three autumnal colored flowers in glass vases. Six large buffet tables were set at the front of the room and were overflowing with food.

"Look at the amount of food," Sage said.

"Everyone in the town really came through.

Every bit of it has been donated by Gerald's and Ella's friends and family. And there is more in the kitchen to refill the plates as they empty," Sarah replied.

"Ella was really loved by the locals. She sat on several committees in the town and served as a selectman up until ten years ago when she retired to head up the church choir."

"Yes, and she did wonders with the choir here. We had no males singing until Ella recruited them from the local theater company. Now it's a joy to listen to them on Sunday mornings," Sarah said.

"I haven't been down here since they redid the sanctuary," Sage said. "I love what they did to it."

"That's my favorite area," Sarah said, pointing to the far wall. "They framed all the family pictures taken of the church members all the way back to when the church was built. That wall has all the serving ministers and their families."

"Some of the pictures are in black and white. That makes it even more interesting," Cliff stated. "I'm going to go look for my grandparents' picture."

They wandered up and down the rows of pictures stopping when they recognized family members. Sage didn't have any family church members as her mother was the first one who started coming to the church when her original church burnt down and wasn't rebuilt.

"Cliff! Come look at this!" Sage called out excitedly.

"What am I looking at?"

"Check out the name of the head of this family."

"Bryant Winters. I think we just found our Bryant and he's Lucy's father," Cliff stated.

"This does complicate things in trying to find answers. He died over twenty years ago according to the plaque," Sage replied. "We have even more reason to talk to Lucy tomorrow. Maybe she knows why her father went to see Roger."

"Right now, we have to get upstairs for the service," Cliff said, checking his watch for the time.

"Save me a seat. I'll be right up," Sarah said as they walked by her.

Lucy was standing at the back of the church checking on her flower arrangements. Sheriff White was standing at his wife's side at the front of the church. He looked tired and drained. The chapel was packed and there was standing room only at the side and back of the church. The minister escorted Gerald to his seat and returned to the podium.

An hour later the service ended. It was a beautiful ceremony laced with wonderful music and many locals speaking about Ella and how she touched their world. Even Sage's mom got up and spoke while choking back her tears. Several times Sage found tears rolling down her cheeks and Cliff took her hand to comfort her. His warm touch was welcoming and helped Sage to calm down.

"Ladies and gentlemen, there will be a receiving line at the back of the church and then Gerald has asked that I invite everyone downstairs for lunch. Please don't forget to sign the visitor's book on your way out," the minister said from the back of the church.

"That was beautiful," Sage said as they waited in the receiving line to offer their condolences to the sheriff.

"Now we have a ton of work ahead of us at the farm," Cliff stated. "But, first, all that food downstairs is calling my name."

They reached the sheriff who smiled when he saw them. Cliff shook his hand and Sarah gave her old friend a hug. Sage reached in for a hug next when the sheriff whispered something in her ear.

"Any luck on finding the name of the person who killed Roger Perkins?"

Shocked that he would ask her something like that

at this place and time, she whispered back that they were getting closer to a solution.

"Cliff, I'll be over to the farm after this is over to help with the hayride set-up," the sheriff said.

"You don't have to do that," Cliff replied.

"I know I don't have to, but I want to. I have to keep busy and besides, it is benefiting the 4H which was one of Ella's pet projects," he said, smiling. "And you, missy, we need to have a conversation regarding your progress. I will be returning to work on Monday and will be heading to your house for an update."

"Gerald, I thought we agreed you would take a few weeks off," Sarah stated.

"I can't just sit at home. It would be better for me to be out doing something and Ella would have wanted me to go back to the work I love."

"If you think that is what is best for you," Sarah replied. "The selectmen will be glad to see you back at work although Andy has done a great job stepping in while you have been out."

"I heard. I was afraid I might lose my job getting ousted by someone younger," he said, jokingly.

"Never happen," Sarah replied, squeezing his hand. "We'll see you downstairs."

Sage couldn't wait to speak with the sheriff and tell him what they had found so far regarding Roger's murder. Sarah disappeared into the kitchen once they were downstairs. Sage and Cliff filled their plates and took a seat at the table nearest the family portraits. The sheriff didn't eat much but instead visited from table to table thanking everyone for coming.

They finished eating and Sage went into the kitchen to tell her mother they were leaving for the farm. Cliff wanted to get there ahead of any other volunteers who were going to start arriving. Sarah insisted they each take a plate of food with them. Cliff loaded a plate with lasagna and meatballs and Sage helped herself to a variety of desserts. His parents promised to be back at the farm shortly.

Volunteers were trickling in and by two o'clock, there were more than enough people for the jobs that needed to be completed. Cliff and his dad had set up a display chart of what needed to be done and would write each person's name on the chart as they headed off to a particular area.

"This is going to be awesome," Cliff said as he and Sage walked the hayride path at the end of the day.

"I can't believe we had enough people to get the set-up almost complete in one day," Sage replied.

"There is very little left to do, mostly electrical work that my dad is going to be working on tomorrow. And we have twenty more people this year than we did last year who want to participate and be spooky characters along the ride."

"This celebration grows every year which is a good thing for the chosen charities," Sage replied.

"So, what character are you going to dress as?" Cliff asked, grabbing for her hand.

"None. Gabby and I are going to man the ticket booth. Speaking of Gabby, I wonder why she wasn't at the service today," Sage said. "I haven't talked to her since we went to the barn the day she found the skeleton. I need to give her a call and find out what's going on."

As they walked along, they stopped at each area and checked out the scene. There were fourteen in all, each one that would feature a different Halloween character. There were vampires in coffins, werewolves who would come out of the woods and chase the wagon, witches stirring a large bubbling caldron along with several cemeteries that would sprout ghosts and zombies.

The hayride would last about twenty minutes and stop at each area. It would cost five dollars for adults and three dollars for kids under twelve. It was a family orientated event so there would be no blood and gore which would scare the younger viewers.

"I think once the strobe lights, purple lights, and spotlights are hooked up it will be awesome," Cliff said as they neared the end of the path. "Dad and I are going to pick a mess of pumpkins and pile them up near the ticket booth. We will offer them for two dollars apiece and have tables and chairs set up if the customer wants to carve them before they head home. The store will have hot cider and donuts for sale as well as apple bobbing for the kids."

"It sounds like you have everything covered. It should be an awesome night," Sage replied. "You may have to start running the event more than one night and not just on Halloween."

"Dad said the same thing. He was thinking three nights next year, but we have to check with the people who don the makeup and costumes to see if they would be willing to extend their time. If they say yes, then it will be for three nights."

"That's better if you think about it. The line is usually a mile long for the hayride and you always have to run overtime to get everyone through who has bought a ticket."

"I think it would be less busy on Halloween night if we offered the two nights before. People can take their kids trick or treating and attend parties instead of wasting the whole night standing in line," Cliff replied.

"It would mean more money for the charities also."

"Yes, it would and for the farm. The seedlings for the Christmas trees are going to cost a pretty penny and I would love to have the money already set aside and not have to take it out of the existing farm budget."

"Cliff! Sage! Mom has supper on the table. Come on," Cliff's dad yelled from the porch of the farmhouse.

"I guess I am invited to supper," Sage said, smiling.

"Let's eat and then I'll run you home."

"The cats are used to eating an hour ago. I'm sure I will be attacked as I go through the door."

The evening was spent laughing at the stories Cliff's parents were telling Sage about their son when he was a little tyke. Sage offered to help clean up after supper and was politely but firmly told no. Instead, Cliff brought the truck around to bring her home. She thanked his parents for the delicious supper and said goodbye.

Motorboat and Smokey were sitting in the bay

window watching for her. They started meowing loudly when she got out of the truck.

"Man, they can sure make a racket. The windows are all closed, and you can still hear them outside," Cliff said, laughing.

"They quiet down as soon as they have food set in front of them," Sage replied.

"Did you leave the light on in your workshop when we were in there earlier?" Cliff asked.

"No, why? Are they on?"

"Stay here," he replied, heading for the shop.

"Cliff!" Sage yelled.

"No one's here now but someone was earlier," he replied. "They did a job on your shop."

Sage entered her workspace and gasped. The hasp holding the padlock on had been pried from the wall and the inside had been turned upside down.

"We know what they were looking for. They must have seen us with the journal through the window. Luckily they didn't see me at the safe because the workbench hasn't been touched."

"Don't touch the journal tonight. Someone may be watching us right now," Cliff warned.

"I'm not even going to worry about the shop being open for the night. I'll close the door the best I can and then fix the hasp in the morning. I just don't understand it. What is in that journal that is so important to someone? We must have missed something," Sage said.

"I don't know but let's get you inside and lock the door."

Sage waved to Cliff and shut off the Halloween lights that decorated her front porch. The cats followed her, talking a blue streak until she fed them. While they ate, Sage walked around the first floor making sure every window and door was locked and the first floor was secured. She went to bed feeling safe in her own house.

Cliff called her early the next morning to say he had to stay at the farm and attend to some business. Sage finished her coffee and set out for the flower shop to speak with Lucy about her father.

She parked in the rear parking lot and walked around the back of the shop. Passing by the window behind Lucy's desk, she saw the elderly woman sitting at the desk with her face buried in her hands. In between her fingers she was clutching a gold pocket watch. She slipped back to her car without being noticed.

I have to check the journal for dates. I'll be back Lucy.

Sage drove home as fast as the law would allow.

She scoped out the area around the workshop, seeing no one she retrieved the journal and locked herself in her van. Flipping to the last entry in the journal her thoughts had been confirmed.

The last entry in the journal was made on October twenty-ninth, the day Lucy's father went to see Roger and he was never heard from again. Today's date was October twenty-ninth. He must have killed Roger, either by accident or on purpose and then taken the missing gold watch. She didn't know how Lucy ended up with it and wouldn't know until she asked her. She dialed her cell phone.

"Sheriff White, this is Sage. I believe I know who killed Roger Perkins. Would you meet me at Lucy's flower shop? Great, I'll see you shortly."

CHAPTER SEVEN

"Hello, Annie," Sheriff White said as they entered the flower shop. "Is Lucy here?"

"She's out back doing paperwork. Do you want me to let her know you are here?"

"No, thank you. We'll go out back to talk to her," the sheriff replied.

Lucy looked up as the duo walked up to the desk. Her eyes were swollen and red.

"Today is the day Roger died, isn't it, Lucy?" Sage asked. "According to the journal, a person named Bryant was the last person to see him alive."

"Is the journal talking about Bryant Winters, your dad?" the sheriff asked.

"You found the journal?" she asked, sighing deeply.

"I did. And today's date, all those years ago, was the last entry made. The day your dad went to confront Roger Perkins about your affair."

"Who did you send to retrieve the journal from Sage's house?" the sheriff inquired.

"I didn't send anyone, I swear," she replied.

"You have the missing watch?" Sheriff White asked.

"I do," she said, opening the drawer and pulling it out.

"Did your dad give it to you?" Sage asked.

"No, I received it in the mail several weeks later after Roger left without me. I mean after he was killed and left in the barn."

"It was mailed to you?" Sage repeated.

"It was. There was no note or anything with it. I knew how much it meant to my Roger, so I kept it close to me without telling a soul that I had it," she replied, holding the watch to her chest. "I didn't care who sent it. It gave me comfort just to possess it."

"Did your dad tell you about his meeting with Roger?"

"He did," she replied, bursting out crying.

"Tell us what he said, Lucy," the sheriff requested.

"He said he walked into the barn and Roger was

talking to himself and pacing. He had just made up his mind to stay with Marie and didn't know how to tell me. Then my dad said I told you so. Marie had talked to Roger and told him she still loved him and always would. Roger had a whole week to think about her words and he made the decision to stay with his wife. My dad said he made me look like a fool around town, and I would never get a husband when everyone found out he strung me along and then dumped me."

"So, Bryant Winters killed him out of anger at what he had done to you?" the sheriff asked.

"No, you have it all wrong," Lucy sobbed.

"You went to the farm and killed Roger, didn't you Lucy?" Sage asked, kneeling in front of the woman and taking her hand. "Was it an accident?"

"Yes, I did. After three years of promises, he backed out a week before we were to leave together. I was devastated when my dad told me. I had to go hear it for myself, from his lips."

"Tell us what happened," the sheriff said, softly.

"Marie always had business meetings at the church on Sunday nights. I drove to the farm and Roger was out in the barn. I don't think he wanted to see me after dealing with my dad earlier in the day. We got into a fight. He told me he was staying with

Marie and that I was to go on with my life and forget about everything that happened between us."

"That infuriated you, didn't it?' Sage asked.

"It did. How do you forget about three years of your life and someone you love with every ounce of your being? I saw the two satchels sitting on a desk and it made me even madder knowing how close we had come to spending the rest of our lives together."

"Then what happened?"

"He was writing something in his journal. He turned his back on me and told me to leave the property before Marie came home and saw me there. Before I knew what happened I picked up a fireplace poker and hit him with it. He collapsed and I panicked."

"Did you put him in the chest by yourself?" the sheriff asked.

"I did, but it took me a long time to do. I closed and locked it and piled all kinds of stuff around the chests."

"And you took the satchels when you left?"

"I knew if anyone asked I could always say he dropped them off before he disappeared. It would look like we were still leaving together. After a while I hid them up in the attic at the shop and forgot about them."

"Under the circumstances I think you need to return the money to Marie, don't you?" Sage suggested.

"What money?" the sheriff asked.

"The money Roger took out of his bank accounts to bring with us to start our new lives together," Lucy replied. "Sage found it in the lining of one of the satchels. It's been sitting up in the attic all these years and I didn't even know it was there."

"Have you ever told anyone else about that day?" Sage asked.

"No, not a word. My dad and I were the only two who knew Roger had changed his mind. I even went to the motel for three days to make it look like I was waiting for him to join me. My dad said I had to protect his good name and by staying at the hotel it would look like Roger had run off on both Marie and me."

"I think we need to go down to the station and file a formal report on Roger Perkins' death. Can you ask Annie to close up the shop?" the sheriff requested.

"I can, and Sheriff White, it's actually quite a relief to tell someone what happened that day. It has been wearing heavily on me my whole life."

Lucy went to talk to Annie.

"Someone else knew Roger Perkins was dead.

That same someone went into the barn after Lucy left and snagged the watch out of the chest."

"But why would they mail it to Lucy?" the sheriff asked.

"Maybe they wanted her to feel guilty the rest of her life because of what she did," Sage replied. "Think about it. There is only one person who would have been at the farm and maybe saw what happened."

"Marie Perkins!" the sheriff said.

"We need to talk to Marie," Sage replied.

The sheriff spoke into his shoulder radio. They went to the front of the shop and Lucy was ready to go. Annie was crying, upset at the fact Lucy had told her what was going on and that she had to leave.

"Andy is going to escort you down to the station," the sheriff said. "I have some business to take care of and then I will join you at the station."

"May I take the watch with me?" Lucy requested.

"I think it would be better if you left it here, safe in the drawer where it's been all these years," the sheriff replied. "Andy's here."

"Are you going to handcuff me?" she asked fearfully.

"I don't think we need to do that. Why? Are you

planning on trying to escape on the way to the station?"

"No. You're just teasing me, aren't you?"

"I am. Keep your chin up. Things look bad now, but we'll see what happens," the sheriff said, closing the door to the cruiser.

"Sage, do you think Lucy would mind if I closed the store early?" Annie asked as the cruiser with her boss in it drove away. "Like right now?"

"I'm sure she won't mind, considering," Sage replied.

"Good, I don't think I could face all the questions. Excuse me while I lock up," Annie said, disappearing into the flower shop.

"Do you want to ride with me or take your van to Marie's house?"

"I'll take my van in case you have to take Marie in for questioning," Sage replied.

Marie was in the barn when they arrived.

"Still looking for the money and the journal?" Sage asked, standing at the door.

"Oh, you startled me. Why do you and your boyfriend insist on sneaking up and spying on people?"

"You mean like the way you spied on Lucy the night she killed your husband?" Sage replied.

Marie stopped what she was doing and stared at Sage.

"I'm sure I don't know what you are talking about."

The sheriff stood back and let Sage take the reins.

"Yes, you do. You came in after Lucy left and took the watch out of the chest. Why did it take you three weeks to mail it to her?" Sage asked. "Were you going to keep it as a reminder of Roger and then you changed your mind?"

Marie plopped down on a nightstand next to her.

"Did you see her kill Roger?"

"No, I watched through the window as she was trying to stuff him in the chest. She was crying hysterically the whole time and professing her love for him. She was a wreck."

"So, you don't know if she did it or someone else did it?" Sage asked.

"Where are you going with this, Sage?" the sheriff asked.

"No, I don't. I just assumed she did it."

"Why did you wait so long to send her the watch?"

"I figured Roger had been planning on staying with me and the watch might bring the poor woman some comfort," Marie replied. "It wasn't done out of spite. It was done out of sympathy."

"How did you know Roger was staying with you and not leaving with Lucy?"

"My husband told me."

"No, he didn't. He had just made up his mind when Bryant Winters came to face him. The only way you would have known that is if you had witnessed the conversation between the two men."

Marie stared at Sage. Her shoulders sagged and she teared up.

"Lucy didn't kill Roger, did she? Bryant Winters did, and Lucy has shouldered the blame all these years to protect her father and the family name."

"Yes, her father killed my husband. Lucy showed up before I could call anyone. She was hysterical. I watched her struggle to lift the heavy body into the chest and then she kissed his forehead before she closed the lid. She really did love him, and I was furious at what he had put her through."

"Why didn't you call someone after Lucy left?"

"Because I knew her father would convince Lucy into taking the blame for the murder. It was all about family status and his name. That was all he cared about and she would have done anything to make him pay a little attention to her."

"So, you kept it a secret all these years to protect Lucy?" the sheriff asked.

"If I had called anyone, he would have laid the blame on her and walked away without any regret that he ruined her life. Back then women were still second-class citizens, and it would have been her father's word against mine and Lucy's word. He was a deacon in the church and a selectman at the time. Who do you think they would have believed?"

"Lucy denied sending anyone to try to steal the journal. It was you, wasn't it?" Sage asked.

"It was me. I thought if I could destroy the journal then Lucy's secret would be safe. I didn't care that people thought I did it all these years. I knew I didn't and that was all that mattered to me. I will reimburse you for any damage caused. I'm sorry."

"People need to know the truth. Bryant Winters has been dead a long time and neither you nor Lucy need to take the blame anymore," Sage stated.

"Lucy is down at the station confessing to the murder as we speak. You need to accompany me down there and tell Lucy she doesn't have to feel guilty anymore. You need to convince her to admit to the truth about her father," Sheriff White said.

"I don't understand. If you knew the body was in

here why did you open the barn to us? Didn't you figure it would be found?"

"Truthfully. My mind is not what it used to be. I have early onset dementia and totally forgot my Roger was in here," Marie admitted. "That is why I asked Cliff to suggest a good attorney. I need to get my affairs in order before I can't even do that."

"I'm so sorry to hear that," the sheriff replied.

"It doesn't matter about me. The important thing is the truth will come out and Lucy can now live a guilt-free life. Shall we go so I can talk to Lucy and tell her it is over, and she needs to tell the truth?" Marie said, standing up. "May I take my own truck? I'd like to drive while I still can."

"Yes, I'll meet you at the station," the sheriff replied. "Go directly there."

"I will. It's time Lucy got her life back. She's paid her dues."

They watched Marie drive away.

"How did you know? How did you know Lucy didn't do it?"

"It was a hunch actually. It was the way she said her dad told her his good name had to be protected. Why would he say that if he hadn't done it?"

"Good catch. Will you lock up? I'm going to the

station and clear this matter up after forty plus years of speculation," he said, climbing into his cruiser.

"Sheriff?" Sage said.

"Yes?"

"It's good to have you back," Sage said, smiling.

"It's good to be back," he replied, closing the car door.

CHAPTER EIGHT

"Here's to another successful event at the Fulton Farm," Sage said, raising her wine glass in a toast.

"The 4H will be receiving a check for seven thousand dollars next week. That should keep some of their programs going for the next year," Cliff replied, joining the toast with his beer.

"And I'm glad our missing Gabby has returned. Do me a favor, best friend. Next time you go out of town a quick call would be nice," Sage lectured her.

"I'm sorry. My mom had to go to Massachusetts for a will reading at the last minute and we packed up and left right after the call," Gabby explained.

"I hope it wasn't a close family member," Cliff replied.

"No, it was an old friend of hers from school. It

was weird. She hadn't seen this person since the last class reunion fifteen years ago. He left her a collection of glass paperweights. She said they used to collect them together when they were younger."

There was a knock on the door.

"Trick or treat," a group of children yelled when she opened the door.

"I'm so glad you are here. I was afraid I would have to eat all this candy by myself," Sage said, dumping candy in each bag. "Have fun."

"I can take some of that candy off your hands," Cliff said, chuckling.

"I think the food is ready. Everyone hungry?" Gabby said, returning from the kitchen.

"Let's eat! First a toast," Cliff stated. "To Sage. My gorgeous and smart girlfriend who managed to solve a murder from almost fifty years ago and made another woman's life much happier."

"Here! Here!"

"Now can we eat?" Rory asked. "Chasing around that hay wagon all night has given me quite an appetite."

"And may I say you made quite an impressive zombie," Gabby said to her fiancé.

The group went to the kitchen to eat. The sheriff joined them for a bite to eat and then went back to finish his shift. After dinner, the party moved outside so they could enjoy the lights that had been put up around the yard. Gabby and Rory strolled around walking off their supper.

"Look at the full moon. It's perfect for a Halloween night.," Sage said.

"Perfect night for a perfect life," Cliff replied.

"Our life is pretty perfect, isn't it?" Sage said, sighing and snuggling in next to her boyfriend in the hammock.

"It is, and it will only get better the more time we spend together," he replied.

"That sounds like you are planning for the future, Mr. Fulton,"

"I am, and as long as you are in it, my life couldn't be more perfect."

Printed in Great Britain
by Amazon